HALF

DUNCAN MACLEOD

ISBN-13: 9781973127093

DEDICATION

For Michael G. Page

CONTENTS

ACKNOWLEDGMENTS

This book takes place in a real time and a real place. Many of the characters are purely fictional, while others are based on real people. I'm not free to say which is which, since so much of the book is fiction. If you think you see yourself, you may be mistaken. Similarly, you may be in here so well disguised you'll never figure it out. I would like to thank certain individuals, without whom I would never have made it this far. Whether it was their tarot readings, pink sofas, gem elixirs or their constant love and support, I needed them all in my life. San Francisco in the 1980s was a magical place, and it attracted a lot of magicians, witches, and other experts in the mystical arts. Who better could help a young man "drowning in the waters where the mystics swim"?

CHAPTER ONE - RIDING THE RAILS

Clackety-clack clackety-clack clackety-clack clackety-clack; the sound of the metal wheels rolling across the ties forms the soundtrack to my cerebral meltdown. I'm somewhere between Fremont and Milpitas now. The train doesn't roll; it meanders. The summer sun in the East Bay is beating on my boxcar, turning it into a sauna reeking of Vidalia onions and cow sweat. Outside the car I can smell the acrid Dumbarton Salt Flats commingling with raw sewage.

When I clambered aboard this slow moving train, I had envisioned a romantic journey with plenty of time to nap and snack to the gently swaying beat of the rails. Sadly, the boxcar is not designed for passengers, and the swaying motion is more a series of violent jerks every 200 feet. Lying down has proven to be a big mistake. I'm in danger of vomiting my granola bar. Snacks are out of the question.

Nausea grounds a person. My brain activity is redirected from flights of fancy towards keeping from barfing all over my travel clothes. Right now I'm facing forwards, sitting upright with my back against the rear wall of the boxcar, taking shallow breaths and fanning myself with a folded paper fan made from a discarded YMCA flier. I have a moment to reflect on my situation as I lurch and jerk towards an unknown destination.

The mental fog akin to having my brain ripped out and replaced with milk-soaked cotton balls has lifted since I started at the Schizophrenia Project. The ensuing mental clarity teetered for several delightful moments at the point where my mind and my mood were in that harmonious state doctors call "feeling normal" before toppling over into a freshly mown patch of insanity. The euphoria lasted long enough to get me on board this train, AWOL, with a backpack full of stolen granola bars and a bad case of motion sickness. This is what it's like to withdraw from Prolixin.

I'm aware now the crappy feeling in the hospital was more than half due to the nasty drugs they had me on. I am so much more powerful and aware and capable when I'm not taking them. Yeah, okay so I need to slow down and think before leaping on board moving trains.

Whoosh! A fast-moving train zips past and blows some more fetid diesel dust into my squalid cabin of seasickness. I'm pretty sure I'm in Milpitas now; the train makes a screeching turn towards the West. I smell the junkyard. Outside, a cast-off doorless refrigerator hosts a multi-colored pile of consumer waste in 1960's hues of pink, orange and green. One refrigerator hangs open like the mouth of a dessicated mummy, stained with blackened spinach, spilled milk, and Worcestershire sauce. The egg crate gapes like a jaw full of empty sockets where missing teeth should be.

Here in Milpitas there are still RR Xings without automatic arms. Clanging bells and flashing lights sound their naive warning to motorists. Buses must stop at these crossings and open their doors to listen for trains before proceeding. Parked at one these crossings in an ancient International Harvester trucks sits an old rancher, wrinkled like a piece of nylon stuffed in haste under a mattress ten years ago and just removed. He leans his head against the window of his driver side door. Our eyes connect as I pass by. In that human moment, I can't resist the urge to wave, and he waves back. I'm on Earth; he sees me, and I am part of the great California landscape.

In the middle of an abandoned broccoli field stands a billboard announcing "Stoneridge Estates, Coming Summer 1988." The Silicon Valley, once known as the California fruit bowl, is turning into a wilderness of concrete, cheap stucco and skateboard ramps.

Milpitas fades into Santa Clara. In the distance I can see the mountains of Los Altos and spiny fingers of the triple Ferris Wheel at Great America. It was only three years ago I was enslaved at that godawful amusement park for 3.35 an hour selling a juice-like substance in plastic containers designed to look like the artificial fruit flavor they contained. Grape punch came in a bulbous purple bunch of grapes, orange liquid came in an orange globe. For some reason, fruit punch came in a red ovoid with a green top and was always mistaken for a strawberry. "Is this strawberry juice"? The concerned mother would ask, and I, having heard the question for the 47th time that hour, had learned to nod. No one could tell the difference between artificial strawberry and fruit punch anyway. They wouldn't fire me for my little half-truth, would they? There were no secret shoppers lurking about, ensuring clients of Great America were having the optimum juice buying experience. It was no Disneyland. So I had no real reason to explain, "No, although it looks rather like a strawberry, it's an industrial impressionist interpretation of what a fruit punch would look like if it had grown on a tree."

I connect with the lonely teenager in his polyester uniform, his jaunty newsboy cap perched to one side, selling juice in self-reflexive containers to the masses of sugar-hooked Great Americans. That was me. During the gloomy, lonely summer I could never have imagined after graduation from a fancy prep school I would land in a mental hospital. I had no idea mental illness lurked in the dark recesses of my consciousness. We all listened to Morrissey crooning “How Soon Is Now"? that summer, all of us, and we all felt the same sad isolation, didn’t we? Why aren’t we all in the asylum, and why haven’t we all arrived en masse to ride this train? How did I get here, alone?

Clackety-clack chunk-chunk-chunk. The boxcar lurches again and nausea sweeps over me in a vomitous wave. I guess hobos need their sea legs before attempting to ride these uncomfortable cars. How did I get here? How did I get here? What were the signs? How could I know I would wind up all alone in a boxcar, a diagnosed schizophrenic, queer and nauseated? Was it sports? I hated sports; I never saw the point. Someone was always going to win and someone was always going to lose (usually me) so what was the point in trying? Was that schizophrenia? Was it my love handles formed in fifth grade after a bad case of mononucleosis? Was that the clue I was a future lunatic? I had breasts in junior high and some of the kids called me “titty boy.” Was that why I turned out schizophrenic? Was it because I had to plug my ears and close my eyes during the scariest parts of monster movies? Was it because I was (and still am) afraid of Bigfoot? How could I know it would all end like this? Will I ever get better?

But maybe I already am getting better. I still see aliens on the Number 27 bus, but now I know I’m not supposed to be seeing them. Pens move by themselves all the time, and it isn’t the sign of the end of days. I just have to learn how to filter out all the extraneous messages I receive from unknown voices and I’ll be okay.

Clackety-clack thunk-thunk-thunk. Outside my boxcar are more boxcars, empty cars, underachieving railroad cars. All around, the number of tracks multiplies as my car slows then stops, surrounded like another boxcar in line at the railroad unemployment office. The car jars me when it screeches in reverse for a few hundred yards, and then comes to a stop again.

A few hot fly-stained minutes float by and it occurs to me we're parked somewhere in San Jose.

San Jose is one of those cities you could skip visiting for a whole lifetime, even if you lived a few miles away. Such has been the case in my life. Although I've always wanted to go to the Winchester Mystery House with the ghost of Sarah Winchester howling "Keep building! Keep building"! I have never done so. I know I must have passed through San Jose on my way to a real destination like Santa Cruz, but I have never stopped here. Once I tried to catch a different bus to work at Great America. It left me off in an unfamiliar place which may have been San Jose. That's how lost I am now as I hop from my immobilized boxcar and climb my way to freedom. I'm lost, but not far from home. Home. Will my bed be waiting for me there? Is it even my bed? It's just borrowed, a crash pad in the mental health system. The sun beats overhead; noontime. By now someone from Central City Day Treatment will have called, wondering why I am not attending their mind-numbing Tinkertoy and glue festival. I should be making portraits of Native American faces out of dried kidney beans, macaroni and black yarn right about now. The whole lodge may be in a panic looking for their missing client. I've been gone for hours.

This train yard is surrounded by a high chain-link fence. There are no people around, at least not where I can see them. This is one of those in-between places, where industrial technology holds court and humans are secondary considerations. There are no sidewalks, no paths, no exit, just hundreds and hundreds of railroad tracks. At last a gap in the fence appears and I wriggle my way through onto the street. There's sunshine, warehouses, piles of industrial wreckage, and a lone taco truck.

I approach the owner inside his rolling business, my first

human interaction since this morning when the alien sent me rolling south on the doomed freight train.

"Excuse me sir, can you tell me where the bus is"?

"Mande"? He doesn't understand my English.

"Busco el autobús." Tenth grade Spanish comes flooding back to me.

"No hay." There's no bus. I'm sure the mixture of astonishment and disappointment on my face can be understood universally. He smiles and asks "Por dónde vas"?

"San Francisco" I answer. I won't be finishing my trip to L.A. I have to give up.

"Ahorita me voy a Fremont, cerca el BART Estation. Allí le puedo llevar." How kind, he will take me to the Fremont BART.

I climb aboard his rickety roach coach. Together we reverse my journey, his pots of rendered animal fat and chopped chicken clanging about in the tiny taco kitchen behind us. My Spanish is terrible, so we nod and smile at one another. He asks me, "Usted tiene familia"?

"No, señor. Mi madre y yo, nada más."

"Y cómo qué no, un hombre tan guapo como usted"?

I have to think about it. Why don't I have a family. Well, apart from being a schizophrenic faggot, there's no reason. Will he understand this obvious answer, or did he have motives when he just complimented my looks by calling me guapo? What is this taco vendor thinking? "Soy joven, señor." I blame my lack of wife and kids on my youth.

"Ah. Sí. Todos los güeros esperan hasta la vejez." Yes, whitey waits til he's old. He puts a well worn hand on my knee and pats it and smiles. Taking inventory of the situation, I conclude this kind old man has a hidden agenda. There is a familiar gleam in his eye, and I'm not sure how to handle this. A block further down, I can see the BART sign. At the light, I open my door, hop out, bow and wave.

"Muchísimas gracias, Señor."

"De nada." His smile doesn't fade. I doubt he was coming on to me, but I wanted to be safe. BART is ten paces away; it was time to go anyway.

CHAPTER 2 - INFORMATION

On Ninth Street I worry about what kind of trouble I'm in. Just because a pen moved I decided to throw my whole mental health career out the window. I fucked up. How did I tumble from Ivy League to homeless schizo mental health dropout? And now I'm in such big trouble. A cop car goes up Ninth. They're looking for me. My mother will be real proud when she hears about this. Should I flag down the cop and save them the trouble? Too late. Inside the Furniture Mart I can hear the collective sighs of one hundred frustrated workers looking for a purchase order to complete their paper trails. Across the street is the Friends meeting house. I have always wondered why they chose to put it on such a noisy street, while they sit in silence listening for the still, small voice of God. A lost butterfly floats past me. There isn't a tree, a flower, not even a weed for blocks and blocks. Keep flapping your wings, buddy, you'll find something eventually.

There's the Underground, where just a few months ago me and Donny met with Lola to do some smack. A heavy lead curtain separates my present self from the carefree self of yestermonth. I could no more return to such ease and adventure than a fly could pass through a glass window, and I buzz, crash my frantic wings in a vain attempt to return to the past. "Let go," a voice whispers inside my head, and I fall to the dusty windowsill of the present moment.

At the door to Northeast Lodge, I chicken out and go inside the liquor store instead. Dixie is inside, buying a coke. Her heavy sandals slap hard against the concrete and linoleum floor. I expect her to come running to me and tell me how cops are after me but she's in such a Thorazine daze she just flaps past without paying me the least notice. I buy a bag of barbecue Fritos. They taste good and help settle my upset stomach.

The payphone in the doorway of the liquor store is broken, but it lets you dial directory assistance for free.

I dial 411 and wait for the recorded voice to ask, "What city please?" before speaking.

"I'm sorry ma'am, I'm just scared and I need someone to talk to. Can you talk"? There's a pause while the operator comes on the line.

"I'm sorry sir, but my average handle time per call needs to be 30 seconds or less."

"Well, would you consider praying for me, then"? My question pierces the cold isolated heart of the call center.

"Yes sir, I will. Can I get you the number for anything"?

"No, ma'am, just a prayer."

"God bless you, sir." She disconnects. I love directory assistance.

In my haste to flee Northeast Lodge, I forgot my key in my room, on the dresser near the moving pen, so I have to buzz in. Beep.

"Hi, who's there"? Connie's voice is familiar and comforting.

"Ethan." The door buzzes.

Inside, there are no cops to escort me back to jail. Dixie sees me this time and says, "Come on Ethan, it's time for Deli Project. We're making oatmeal cookies." She climbs the stairs towards the kitchen.

I follow her. Elliott is already wearing his apron and placing potatoes in a series of neat rows. Barbara, the deli project manager, sees me and beams. "There you are! I thought you were in your room. I sent James to get you and he never came back. Listen, we need some potatoes sliced thin for potato chips using this mandolin. Do you think you can handle it if I show you? You have to wear protective gloves, okay"?

I nod, dumbfounded.

In boarding school, they have their shit together. If you were to miss one class let alone a whole day of classes without an excuse, they would have phoned your parents, suspended you from classes, and brought you before the discipline committee – a jury of your peers who would pronounce a judgement upon you for your indiscretion. The mental health system is less organized than Elliott's potatoes.

In the middle of the night, I wake with cramps. There is someone in the upstairs toilet so I have to take the back stairs before my bowels erupt. Outside the paint-smudged window is the Northeast Lodge parking lot on Dore Alley. Shadowy figures dart about; ghosts in a graveyard in some mysterious dance; a mating ritual. Note to self: check out the parking lot one night.

The toilet on the first floor landing is free. On the way back upstairs, I pause to watch the activity out the rear window. The men (for they could only be men) are clad in black leather, shrouded in darkness. Only the occasional flicker of a match, followed by the red glow of a cigar, divides the inky black murk into puddles of light. Who are these black-clad men? Do they know I am watching in the night?

I shiver and return to the pale comfort of my polyester sheets and acrylic blanket. It's 2:45 am and soon the dawn will bring another day filled with far less adventure than the day before.

CHAPTER 3 - MICHAEL G. PAGE

On coffee walk with the crew I hear someone calling my name. "Ethan? Ethan? Is it you"? I pause and the flock of coffee-mad inmates waddles past me. In their wake is Michael Page.

It has been a year since I last saw Michael Page in New York holding court over a gaggle of club kids at Danceteria. His hawk-like features, with the most intense angry eyebrows and a shiny beak of a nose, made him look like he was about to vomit predigested worms into their little squawking mouths. I heard he had fled New York for the warmer pastures of San Francisco, but never saw him until now. He looks the part for this city in his grey dungarees with an East German military bag. No makeup, no homemade fun-fur costumes, just the bare self. What a spectacular inconvenient coincidence it is to run into him here, with all my current posse in tow.

"Ethan, who are all these fabulous hags"?

I blush, stammer, explain "They, uh, they live in the same building as me."

"Girl, I heard all about you from Sister Ekoplasma."

"You did"? I turn a deep shade of embarrassment red.

"They let you walk around? I thought it was a lockdown at General Hospital."

"Uh, no. It's-um-I'm not in the hospital anymore."

"Oh, you're at a halfway house"?

"Three-quarter way house," I correct him.

Michael sniffs and smiles at me. "Going to Café Soma"?

I nod. He hooks his arm through mine and walks beside me towards the café.

"You know, I'm crazier than all you bitches put together. I just haven't let them find out. If they did, they would put me away forever."

Inside the café, Dixie accosts Michael. "Hi, I'm Dixie. What's your name?

"I'm Michael G. Page. Don't forget the G. or you'll fuck up my numerology. Girl, what did you do to those glasses"? He points to the two dots of nail polish at the center of each of her lenses.

"It's to keep my mind focused."

"It's a great look for you, doll." Dixie loses focus, and wanders away to her table. James is in charge of the money. When he sees my unexpected guest he panics. "No, sorry, we don't pay for you, no."

Michael waves two tattered dollar bills in the air. "I've got my own money, piss off."

The cute boy behind the counter gives me an extra-frothy cappuccino and I sit with Michael at our own table, away from the crazies.

"They finally gave me SSI," Michael tells me. "I had to appeal twice but in the end they gave it to me. I'm saving to get my own place."

"Where do you live now"?

"Oh, that's right! You haven't been to my little palace of squalor, have you? I have a room at the Civic Center Hotel. Here's my card." He hands me a homemade business card crafted from a brown paper bag, decorated with glitter. He smiles at me with a faint flicker of friendship. I know the look. It is a safe, non-sexual meeting of the eyes meaning we are friends now. "Call me and we'll go out."

"I have a curfew."

"I'm getting old, bitch. I'll be thirty in November. We'll go early so we can talk to the boys before it gets too crowded and drunk. Just give me a call and we can hang out, you know, during the day or something. Café Flore or wherever."

I study Michael's nervous hands, his angular features. He wears a leather cap pressing his bleach blond bangs into his eyes, no longer teased to outlandish heights.

"What are you looking at, girl"?

"You just look so much more relaxed than you did in New York City."

"I'm old, going bald, it's time to get real."

"You look good."

"Don't lie to me, bitch. I look terrible. Hey, the cute boy behind the counter is trying to get your attention"!

I look across the room, and sure enough, he's waving me over.

"Girl, he's so cute! Go talk to him"!

I should pretend to be a normal person and just go over there and have a word with the handsome man. I dawdle towards the counter. He gives me a big grin.

"Dude, who are these people? Are you with them? You guys are here like every Thursday night."

I hide my inner groan of embarrassment. "I'm not at liberty to say, really. It's part of a secret government experiment." It sounded phony. So phony, in fact, the guy behind the counter laughs and offers me a second cappuccino on the house.

I am hot and anxious as I return to the table with Michael G. Page.

"He's straight. Not interested, just nosy."

Michael frowns. "I think he has the hots for you. He gave you a free cup of coffee, and from where I'm sitting," Michael adjusts his big black horn-rimmed glasses,"I think he's flirting with you and if you would lift your goddamn head you would see what I mean."

I shrug. "No, he's straight. He made sure to mention his girlfriend," I lie.

Michael, unable to resist the flair for the dramatic, points at him and declares, in an outdoor voice, "If he's straight, I will eat my leather hat." A few of the Northeast Lodge residents look up and frown. The boy behind the counter grins and continues to rub a rag up and down the milk steamer in a suggestive manner.

I crumple into my chair. "Can we go? I'm not ready for this."

Michael can see the effect he has had on me, and despite his hard shell, he senses the emotion. He grasps my hand. "Ethan, you are adorable. I keep forgetting you're a sensitive Pisces. Will you forgive me? Come over to my new pad and we'll have a real cup of coffee."

"I have a curfew."

"Saturday morning. Please, it would be an honor to have such a fabulous young gentleman as yourself to entertain in my parlour." Michael is not pervy, and I know it. He genuinely likes me as a friend.

"Saturday morning."

"It's a date! I'll freshen up the place."

CHAPTER 4 - CIVIC CENTER HOTEL

Saturday morning at 9:30 am I walk over to the Civic Center Hotel at 12th and Market. The man behind the counter hates his job. "What can I do for you"?

"I'm here to see Michael G. Page in room 504."

"Michael Page? One second." He raises a black handset to his ear and plugs a jack into the old fashioned switchboard. A few moments pass. I can hear the ring crackling through the ancient receiver.

"You got a visitor." Pause. "That's right. Here." He hands me the receiver.

"Whaaaaat"? Michael's voice wails in despair.

"Hi Michael, it's me."

"Michael G. Page," he corrects me, "Who in the fuck is this"?

Before I can answer, he slams the receiver down.

I hand the receiver back to the front desk clerk.

"Is he on his way down"?

"Yes," I lie.

"Have a seat over there. I'm sure he'll be down." He gestures to a lobby festooned in ferns, with a grimy couch upholstered in a bamboo-theme. An empty bird cage hangs from a hook in the ceiling. Drowsy, I plop on the couch.

The next thing I know, the hotel clerk is shaking me awake. "Hey, your friend is on the line."

I walk back to the reception desk and take the receiver.

"Ethan, doll-face, is it you"?

"Yeah."

"What on earth are you doing here at this godforsaken hour of the morning. You disturbed my beauty rest"!

I must have been asleep for a while, according to the lobby clock. "It's eleven a.m. There isn't much morning left."

"Touché. Come on up. I didn't have time to clean the place, so don't judge me."

"You have to come and get me."

"Let me talk to the prissy bitch behind the counter."

I hand the receiver back to the front desk clerk. "He wants to talk to you."

After a few minutes of back-and-forth chatter on the topics of hotel policy and human decency, the front clerk waves me up. "Fifth floor."

The Civic Center Hotel elevator has one of those metal sliding gates which always makes me think my brooch will be caught in its spokes and I will choke to death like an Italian horror movie villainess. The elevator buttons are replacements of the originals, but they have worn away again from repeated use. I have to count to be sure I pick the fifth floor. I clutch at my throat as the car lurches upward.

Room 504 is not in sequence. I wander past 502, 503, 505, and far off in the distance I hear Michael cry out "Ethan, over here"! Room 504 is wedged between room 522 and room 513. Michael stands at his door in a pink terry cloth robe and untied combat boots.

It's tiny, the smallest room in the building. It's not much bigger than my single dorm room was at John Jay, except it has a bathtub, a sink, and a toilet tucked away behind a door.

Like me, Michael G. Page is not a good housekeeper. His room is piled high with hoards of clothing, fabric, shoes; a rat's nest. Every surface is covered with clutter. But it's beautiful, artistic clutter. Thumbtacked posters from Straight to Hell Night at Danceteria…Hand painted fabric…T-shirts, socks, and underwear. It's an artist's lair. I feel at ease. He makes his bed while talking to me.

"I completely forgot we had a coffee date, Ethan. I should have specified what I meant by Saturday morning. My morning starts later. It's really more like 1pm. But no matter, here, sit down." He pats his bedspread, and a cloud of glitter rises and falls. "I'll get the coffee started."

Below the sign 'No cooking devices allowed,' Michael has created a makeshift kitchen consisting of an electric hot plate on a tiny tv tray. From behind a Rainbow Grocery shopping bag he pulls out an aluminum espresso maker. It comes in two halves. He disappears for a while into the bathroom to rinse out the stains of yesterday's coffee.

"I like your place, Michael. It's so cozy."

"I know, it's surprising what you can still get in this town for $400.00 a month. It doesn't leave a lot for food, but it's a roof over my head and I just love it. I was paying twice as much to live in a broom closet in Manhattan. They had a twin mattress crammed in there, and I just fit. Here in San Francisco, a queen can get a lot more for her money." Michael emerges from the Lilliputian bathroom with the coffee pot, spilling a few drops of water as he shuffles back to the kitchen. It is still stained, but in a permanent way.

Michael scoops and packs the Medaglia d'Oro coffee into the strainer and screws the assembly together. "Without my coffee, I can scarcely move. In five minutes, I will be human again."

As we sip the bitter brew, black, no sugar, Michael asks questions. "How long were you in the hospital for"?

"It was about three months, but it felt like a couple of years."

"I would have died. How did you survive"?

"I guess I didn't really have a choice." I pause to think about it. "I am still a bit surprised to be out, really. I can barely tie my fucking shoes."

Michael cackles with glee. "It was all those nasty drugs they were giving you. Are they still giving you that shit"?

"Maybe, but I think it's a placebo because I don't feel it anymore."

"Why would they give you a placebo? It doesn't make any sense."

"I'm part of a study called the Schizophrenia Project." There is a long, long pause. Michael bursts into laughter like a deranged stroke victim. He can't stop laughing, and neither can I.

"The Schizophrenia Project? What a glorious name for an industrial band"!

"I wish. It's a bunch of old ladies with clipboards."

"Girl, you need to start a new project. It sounds tired."

I realize it has been a long time since I felt this comfortable talking to someone. Michael accepts me. He pours us each another dribble of coffee. "Shall I start another pot"?

"No, I'm fine."

"Let me fuss over you. You deserve it."

The second batch of coffee has me a anxious, but it's outweighed by the joy of bonding with a new friend. Michael pulls a blue pouch out of his robe pocket. "Want a cigarette."?

"Yes please, but what kind is it"?

"Drum. Honey, on my budget, this is the only way to smoke. They give you too much tobacco, so it's really a lot more than 40 cigarettes if you spring for some extra papers."

Michael deftly rolls me a cigarette and another for himself. They taste great, like the inside of a favorite pair of shoes mixed with grape nuts. The smoke is thicker than regular cigarette smoke…or it's just the coffee making me see things that aren't there.

"So of course you got SSI."

"No, I got rejected."

"They always reject you the first time. You have to reapply. You deserve it child. After what they put you through, they owe you."

I'm not sure who "they" are, but he has a point. It would be a good idea for me to get SSI. A steady income, enough to pay for a hotel room somewhere. I can't stay living in the mental health system forever, can I?

Michael is a fountain of information on Social Security and the mental health system. "Girl, if you stick around long enough to transfer to a halfway house, afterwards they have these apartments where you can live for next to nothing! I applied to live in them but there's a waiting list a mile long. If you come from the halfway house, you are first priority."

"I don't know, I dropped out of college. I don't like being stuck somewhere."

"It's worth it. College takes four years. A halfway house is just three months, and you're home free. How many more months do you have to stay in that - what was it - 2/3 house"?

"3/4. Another few weeks."

"Do it girl, trust me. You won't regret it."

After a while, Michael yawns. "You woke me up too early! It's time for my afternoon nap. Get out"!

Walking back to Northeast Lodge, The same sad sinking feeling creeps back in. Talking to Michael, I am a normal human being. He laughs, he makes me laugh…Dixie just stares at me with those cold dead eyes through her lenses painted with nail shellac. Nobody gets me there. Except for Connie. But she's not a patient, so she can’t be a friend.

CHAPTER 5 - FASCINATING

My escapade on the train got me thinking - there's not any real record keeping going on. If I don't go to day treatment, who will know? I decide to test out my theory. Elliott doesn't have day treatment because his insurance doesn't cover it, so he has to leave the house each day and find something to do between 9am and 2pm. He has part time work at a bakery, but today is his day off.

"Elliott, where are you going today"?

"The Electric Theater on Market. Two movies for two bucks. Why"?

"Mind if I tag along"?

"Don't you have day treatment"?

"Nah, they kicked me out." A white lie.

"Well, you got two bucks"?

We walk together to Market Street and hang a right. The Electric Theater is covered in shiny black tile. Its marquee is lopsided, so the letters slide towards the front, cramming together. Today's double feature is 'HELLRAISERNIGHTMAREONELMSTREET3.' Once we are inside the theater, Elliott insists on sixth row center.

The place is empty, so I see no reason to object. "It's the best seat in the house. You'll see what I mean."

Indeed, sixth row center is the best fucking place to sit ever. The sound is perfect, the screen is not too close, not too far. Elliott is a smart guy.

The movie unfolds too fast for me. My mind is still having trouble staying focused, so I don't get why the Cenobites are after the guy. The soundtrack drowns in the voices hollering at the screen. Downtown Movie palaces attract a boisterous bunch, even during the daytime. Rather than try to follow the plot, which is painful, I'm just relaxing in the seat and letting the surrounding chaos become a bubble. It's all around me, and I'm just sitting inside the bubble where the chaos can't reach. At times, every moment of every day is an agonizing bamboo shoot under my fingernails. Right now, it's bearable. I can see why Elliott comes here to escape.

After the double feature, we walk back along Market Street. There is a storefront called "Fascination." It has been around since between the wars. Inside is a line of stools like you find at a carnival water gun attraction. Instead of shooting water into a clown's mouth, the patrons of Fascination are rolling rubber balls along a glass covered wooden grid of holes. The holes have numeric values from 3 to 100. The goal is to reach 500 points before your fellow players. It reminds me of skee ball, but it's flat, with no ramp and no clear path to earn the higher scoring points. An announcer with a gentle, bored voice compliments the players in turn as they score above ten points at a time. Whenever someone hits the hundred hole, the announcer rings a bell. As the top two players are in the home stretch, it becomes a horse race. The dull voice is more animated, the players bang on the glass as if it would bring the rubber ball back to them faster.

Elliot chuckles. "You want a play a few rounds"?

"What do you win"?

"Nothing."

"Not even tickets to redeem for plastic spider rings"? This is odd.

"Nope. The players just play for the thrill of it, I guess."

The business model sounds flawed to me. I can't see how they can keep people coming back to roll a senseless rubber ball for no reward of any kind. And yet there are over a dozen chairs, all but two occupied by Edward Hopper crackpots.

I ask Elliott, "Why do people play"?

"Adrenaline."

"How much does it cost"?

"A quarter a game."

The announcer's dull dry voice complements the flickering fluorescent lights. "And number three just rolled a twenty. Congratulations, number three. Number six just dropped a fifteen, nice job number six."

I could see how the soothing voice and the repetitive motion could be a nice draw in and of themselves. It's like those people who play pickup games of basketball in the park for no real reason other than to play. Several of the people playing look as if they've spent time at Northeast Lodge. A few grubby jackets and stained newsboy hats, a bleach blond lady with a craggy face and a smoldering cigarette dangling from her overpainted lips. Lonesome creeps in as I watch the Fascination players roll their sixes and tens.

"Well, how about it"? Elliott is keen to play.

"Not today, Elliott. Thanks for showing me."

"Aw. come on, Ethan. Just give it a try. I got a few quarters."

It looks pretty pointless to me, but I shrug and accept two quarters from Elliott.

"Just two games and we'll go," he promises.

I sit at number seven, wedged between the craggy-faced blonde on six and a homeless-scented gentleman with a fedora, tweed coat and a grey beard on eight.

The last game has wrapped - a bell rings indicating a winner. The collective groan is something I recall from Bingo matches at summer camp.

"Ladies and gentlemen," the barker whispers, "game 117 will start in 60 seconds. All players insert your quarters now."

I put my quarter in the slot and crank the wheel. A lone rubber ball falls into the well at my lap level. I give it a test roll over the row of holes, and it falls into a hole labeled "two points," while at the same time, an alarm goes off.

"Number seven, you are disqualified from this round." Looking around the room, I can see the glower of several angry players. It would appear this is a faux pas.

"It's his first time, he didn't know, you didn't say anything about waiting." Elliott speaks in my defense.

"It's right there on the rule board." The barker points with a long stick to rule three, which states "No practice rolls. Rolling prior to commencement of the game is grounds for immediate disqualification." This only further convinces me the game is a load of horse shit. "However, we will overlook it." He pushes a plunger and my rubber ball is released back to the lap well.

"I'm sorry. I didn't know, really."

"Tsk. Tsk. We are about to begin. Silence please. Fascination requires intense concentration." The barker looks at his watch, then rings a bell. "The games have begun." The room fills with the sound of beeps and whirs as the players roll their balls."

"Ten points for number thirteen. Lucky roll, thirteen" The barker continues his soft monotonous droning of praise. "The first to 500 wins the game."

I roll the ball, which drops down a three-point hole. This is going to take a while. I sigh with boredom, and the craggy faced blonde shushes me without looking away from her game. I roll the ball again, and this time it spins past the giant three-point holes towards the smaller holes for higher points. It drops down the twenty-point hole."

"Twenty points for number seven. Luck is with number seven." I can see how a compliment from this dry, unloving old man on the microphone could be a source of motivation for lonesome people like myself. The game drifts along, and I grow numb from the endless repetition of rolling the ball. It prefers the three-point holes; I can see my score is not advancing. Then, just by chance, I make it past all the holes in the way and it falls into the one-hundred hole."

"One hundred points for number seven. Luck is with number seven." And he rings the bell. Other than the bell, it's the same basic praise as I got for twenty. Hmmm, this is pretty boring. I try to repeat the move, but the ball overshoots the hundred and lands in the three-point holes behind it. This is pinball without any flippers or bonus features. It's skee ball with no rewards. It is a grim, ghastly emporium of boring repetition for the isolated city dwellers seeking comfort from an otherwise random world. Then the bell rings.

"Congratulations number eight. You have reached five-hundred." All the rubber balls stop as they are caught and held by the game board.

"Shit." The craggy faced blonde on six was at 488 points when my tweedy-bearded neighbor won. He beams; she scowls at him in hatred. I hope they don't fight.

"Game 118 will start in four minutes. Restrooms are next door at the Starlight Room. No one leaves, glued to their stools. Bathrooms are for suckers. I notice I was only at 230 points at the point they stopped the game. It's a game of skill, and my hand-eye coordination, which was pretty bad most of my life, is dreadful while I am on these meds. Elliott strolls over to chat.

"Two-hundred thirty? Come on Ethan, you can do better than that"!

"Why? What's the point"?

My question stumps Elliott. In truth, there must not be an answer, but he makes an eloquent sidestep. "It's not about a point, Ethan, it's about the thrill of victory, and the satisfaction of knowing you did your very best."

I am reminded of the time I joined the junior varsity tennis team at boarding school. No one would play with me, because I didn't care if I hit the ball or not. I was certain I would miss, so I didn't even try unless it came right to me. Coach Stott asked me to leave the team; I took ballet instead. The driving force of competitiveness is anathema to my constitution. Perhaps it is a symptom of schizophrenia. I like to do well in academic subjects, because I know I can. Sports is pointless. I am afraid of the ball, I get winded running the quarter mile, and I can't aim. I throw like a girl, and I run like a pregnant woman. Combined with my poor hand-eye coordination and my aforementioned lack of desire to succeed, and there you have it. A loser.

Fascination is about hand-eye coordination and nothing else. Combined with a desire to win, it must produce some kind of high for the people playing. For me, it creates low-level anxiety and crushing boredom. With no reward at the end, it promises to be an existential nightmare of a game. Huis Clos. It's a treadmill. At least I would be improving myself on a treadmill.

The barker signals the 60 second mark; the players turn their cranks and the rubber balls drop like a bushel of upset apples. I hesitate to play again. There is no meaning or satisfaction to be derived from such a pointless exercise. Still unsure, I place my quarter in the slot and turn the crank. The rubber ball dutifully rolls down the ramp and comes to a stop in the trough at my lap.

I offer it to the craggy faced blonde sitting in number six. She looks at me startled, and the ashes from her dangling cigarette drop into her bosom. The bell rings signaling the beginning of game 118, but number eight is screaming bloody murder. "Cheat! Cheat! He's giving her an extra ball"!

"Fuck you, Erwin, I ain't taking the ball."

I vacate my seat to let the two rivals face one another on their swivel stools. I don't want to get scratched or punched.

"Ladies and Gentlemen, stop game 118, it has been disqualified."

Someone in seat number two says "I just rolled a fucking hundred, what do you mean this is disqualified! Keep playing"!

Sensing the rising tempers in the room, I back away from my seat towards the open doorway onto Market Street.

"It was him! It was number seven"! The body snatchers are after me.

Fuck this, I gotta get out of here. I scramble through the glass double doors, run along Market Street to Ninth and walk the four long blocks to Northeast Lodge. I am winded (of course) but I got away from awful Fascination. I ring the doorbell. Connie's reassuring voice says, "come on in" and she buzzes the door.

Connie is manning the pharmacy. "Connie, I need a PRN of Ativan." In a few minutes, the pill kicks in, and the Fascination panic attack subsides. What an evil place.

Next morning, my counselor David calls me into his office. "This is it," I think, "I'm busted." My truancy is catching up with me. David smokes Capri lights. He puffs away at the thin white stick while he talks to me.

"You got accepted to Conard House."

"Where"?

"Conard House. It's a halfway house in Pacific Heights. The Country Club of the San Francisco Mental Health System."

"I don't remember applying."

"It's not quite like college. Your counselor applies for you. And you got in."

"What if I'm not ready"?

"You're ready."

I let the news sink in. "Where is it again"?

"Fillmore and Jackson, in Pacific Heights. It's a gorgeous mansion; you will love it."

I can't picture myself being ready to leave Northeast Lodge. I still have trouble remembering to tie my shoes. No one here helps me with shoes. It is a safe place to go around feeling disheveled and unkempt. Conard House won't stand for slovenliness.

"Is there a dress code"?

David laughs and draws another long puff from his Capri. "It is not clothing optional, if that's what you mean. No, there is not a dress code. It's a house full of people recovering from grave mental disorders. If you have on flip flops, zipped-up shorts and a tank top, you're meeting the minimum requirement."

"So there's no interview"?

"No. I took care of getting you in there. We're just waiting for a bed to open up."

A deep panic sets in. I can't. I am not ready. A thousand negative thoughts pass through me. David opens his drawer and hands me a pill.

"PRN of Ativan. I figured you might want it."

He is right, of course. He fills a dixie cup from his water cooler and hands it to me. I swallow the Ativan and wait for the panic to subside.

"I wanted to talk to you about something else, Ethan. It's a topic we covered in the past. This is about your mother."

"What about her"?

"She was here at the lodge trying to reach you, and I told her she was not allowed to see you."

"I don't understand. It's my mom."

"Ethan, this won't be easy to hear, and it may make you very angry at me, but you are my client. As my client, I have an obligation to protect you for as long as I am able. Your mother is an extremely dangerous person."

"What, is she a bank robber"?

"An emotional bank robber. I made it part of your treatment plan as an adult, which you are now and without your mother as conservator, which she isn't, she has no right to see you."

"It won't work. She will go ape shit on you."

"It has worked so far. She is not permitted to contact you for as long as you are in my care at Northeast Lodge."

"It isn't fair. I need my mother"!

"Ethan, you need the love and affection of a mother, which is very different. Your mother is both a narcissist and a borderline personality. She is not safe for you to be around."

"How can she be dangerous? I grew up with her! I'm still alive." I am the kind of angry you get when someone talks shit about your mom.

"And where are you alive right now, Ethan? You are living in the mental health system, a basket case, for lack of a more polite term. You had a complete psychotic break, and your life is fucked up right now. That's just happens when you grow up with your mom."

I look at David through the slits of my eyes. Why is he talking shit about Mom?

"Ethan, I told you I had to risk you being angry with me, and I can see you are." He stubs out his Capri and lights another. "I have protected you from her for over two months now." He blows out the first puff of smoke from the second cigarette in the chain.

"She loves me."

"She loves who she can pretend to be when she is with you. Very, very different from actual love."

"I want to go home." I stand up.

"Ethan, you are home. There is nowhere to go right now except to your room. I would prefer if you stay up here with me so we can finish this conversation."

"FUCK YOU FAGGOT"! Tears overflow. I see the look of surprise replaced by acceptance and forgiveness on David's face before I turn and run out of the room. I expect David to call security or come chasing after me, but there are no consequences for my outburst like there might have been in the hospital. I go to my room and let the rage suffocate in the soporific effect of the Ativan. In a few minutes, I hear a knock at my door. It's David.

"Come in."

"I don't need to, I just came to see how you are doing."

"I'm a lot better now."

"I thought you might be. We can finish this conversation at our next meeting."

I'm a dick. "David, I'm sorry I called you the F word."

"Ethan, it was the best thing you did for yourself since you got out of the hospital. Expressing rage is healthy. I am not made of tissue paper - you can yell at me, and I won't fall apart."

This is different. If he was Mom, I would have been slapped silly and grounded for a month. I expect there's repercussions waiting in the wings. "What's my punishment, then"?

David smiles and his little eyes, made smaller by his big glasses, give off a shine.

"Would you like one"? He displays two Capri cigarettes.

"Aren't those women's cigarettes"?

David laughs again. "They provide the illusion that I'm somehow cutting down on my smoking. They taste just like men's cigarettes, I assure you." He proffers the cigarette, and I accept a light from him. We tap our ashes into the wastebasket like firebugs.

"Ethan, you are only just beginning to understand what

it means to be an adult. Adults can tell each other to fuck off. There is no punishment, just varying consequences depending on who you said it to. If I was your boss, you might lose your job. As your counselor, I am delighted you tapped into your rage. I prefer we stay civil while we talk, but if you are angry, let it out with me. It's safe."

This sinks in. I smile and say "Go fuck yourself. Just testing it out."

David chuckles and I can't help but join in the laughter. This is what adults do.

CHAPTER 6 - LET'S SUBMERGE

Today a letter arrives from the Social Security Administration, advising me I have been rejected for SSI a second time.

I run to Connie with the letter to ask her what to do. She tells me to relax. I just have to go to GA tomorrow and apply. I will get GA and my rent at Northeast Lodge will drop to about 15 dollars less than the monthly amount. I won't be eligible for food stamps. It's not ideal, but it is reasonable.

"You should appeal your SSI rejection a second time, too."

"It's too complicated," I reply.

"It's a lot of paperwork, but you will get through it if you're persistent."

Facing off against the Social Security Administration feels too exhausting. I don't tell Connie this, I just file away the guilt of not doing what I should do in order to take care of myself.

Midnight came and went and I am still sitting in bed watching the streetlights flicker. The eerie green glow reminds me of my trip on the spaceship. The earthquakes are back. I can't sleep even if I wanted to. The Underground will be open for another hour. I need to go there to reconnect with my former self. I have nothing to wear but a furry green two-tone cardigan and some grey jeans. They will have to do.

No one in Northeast Lodge is awake at this hour. I know I am breaking curfew, but the freestyle rhythms vibrating out of the club draw me like jungle drums in a voodoo ceremony. Sneaking out is easy. Yeah there's a camera but no one would review the footage unless I were to vanish or commit a murder. The club is just a block north on 9th. The doorman is new. He looks me up and down and says "eleven dollars." I don't have eleven dollars.

"Do you have a handicapped discount"?

"Huh. You ain't handicapped." The song 'Don't Stop the Rock' elicits a mass whoop of joy from inside.

"I'm handicapped, Sir."

"Prove it."

I show my disabled bus pass to the doorman

"What's wrong with you"?

See how I turned the negotiation from one about money to one about my disabled status?

"I have mental problems, " I say. He scrutinizes the bus pass for a second or two then just waves me in.

On the stairs leading to the firetrap dance floor, I bump into Gallon Fairchild. Gallon has to be ten feet tall all swaddled from head to toe in red fun fur with a checkerboard scarf around his giraffe-like neck.

"Ethan, I adore your look! Your monkey fur sweater is hateful"!

"Thanks, Gallon."

I don't know if he was being facetious but he is a pretty straightforward dude from Bakersfield, so I think he means it for real. He grabs my hand.

"Come with me." He leads me back upstairs and introduces me to the new doorman.

"Dimebag, this is Ethan. Ethan shake his hand."

Dimebag smiles. "We met. He's crazy."

"Oh I know! Totally crazy."

Sweet, earnest Gallon Fairchild mistakes the cruel jab for a compliment. "Come on Ethan I want to show you the weirdest fucking thing."

He leads me back out of the club toward Northeast Lodge. I debate whether or not to point out where I live. He passes the Lodge and rounds the corner to Dore Alley. This is where the staff park their cars but it is also something else, the mating dance I saw the other night when I had diarrhea.

Leather and Levi clones are cruising back here. It's scary. I remember Al Pacino in Cruising and my panic button goes off. I don't want to appear scared. I straighten my shoulders; deep breaths.

"Woah, Gallon. You are so right. I can't believe this. It is super cool, très chouette."

He drifts away on the prowl for a man who loves tall young men. I want to crumple into a ball and blow away in the wind; a bedraggled husk of a crustacean.

An older gentleman with an unfortunate pockmarked face approaches me and squeezes my testicles so hard I cry out in pain. "Hot for Jack"! he shouts. Is he Jack? Or does he want to jack off with me? Either way, he's not the man I want to be with today or ever. His leather hat makes him an octogenarian George Michael. Wham, Bam, I am a man. Job or no job…shit! I have to wake early for welfare tomorrow.

I gaze at the crowd of men who spent the 1970's doing things that brought them pleasure, only to learn that they were condemned to death for their hedonism when the 1980's started. I want to feel compassion for these men, but they scare me. They still want to do deadly things. I can't get involved. I don't want to die. There isn't a condom in sight, but there's a lot of condom-worthy activity. This is why so many people keep dying. People my age are getting sick. The drive to have dangerous sex is so powerful, people are willing to throw their lives away. Like a fiend with his dope or a drunkard his wine...where have I heard that? We all know there is no cure. They know how you get it; they know how you give it to others. Yet they want it so bad, they choose to die from fucking.

Standing in this parking lot, I am a swimmer surrounded by black leather sharks. The sharks won't kill each other, but they can easily kill me.

A man with a stinky cigar blows smoke in my face.

"Hey, kid, get on your knees or get lost."

He is a seventies clone. His mustache and his jacket date him. He's old. He must be thirty-five. There's no way he made it through the 1970s without getting AIDS. I look for the tell-tale signs - facial wasting, red face, lesions - no, he's pristine. He reads my mind.

"I'm 100% top; I don't have HIV."

"I'm nineteen, and I don't want to get sick."

"Get lost, then."

He stands, hands on hips, staring me down. I back away and trip over a pair of jacketed clones copulating on the blacktop. My head hits the ground hard. I feel for blood or fractured skull. I'm okay, just a bit dizzy. Nobody comes to help. They are all so wrapped up in their own trip, they don't want to hassle with a fallen toddler.

I give them all the finger and walk away. Nobody notices; nobody cares.

CHAPTER 7 - GENERAL ASSISTANCE

I hit the snooze button so hard, it breaks the alarm. Connie had advised me to go early, but GA opens at 9am, so I figure I'll avoid the rush and head over there at 9:30 am. While this strategy works with banks and the post office, it doesn't work at GA. The line stretches along Bryant Street and turns the corner, heading North on Eleventh Street. I stand in line, trying to avoid making eye contact with thieves and crackheads. About 60% of the line appears to consist of recent releases from San Bruno. There's a presence of imminent danger and intimidation.

There are no cute guys. And there are no cool girls. There's just a sea of bedraggled people whose lives are reduced to waiting in an endless line beside mental patients like me. There is one woman dressed in a white fake fur jacket, with a white dress, white stockings, white nurse shoes, a white macramé hat, and her face is painted white like a clown. She isn't in line - she is walking the line, handing out blessings. Most of the nasty jailhouse dudes shout at her and ask her what the fuck she is doing. The women are just as hostile and unkind. When she reaches me I smile and say, "Hi."

She doesn't speak or smile. She just casts a blessing on me and moves on. One Mexican guy in Dickies shorts with a hairnet, socks to his knees, and tattoos on his face says, "What the fuck are you supposed to be, bitch? Some kind of ghost"? She casts her silent blessing. I bite my tongue, tempted to ask him a similar question.

The woman in front of me is addicted to a stimulant. I don't empirically know this, but her bleached hair appears depleted of vital minerals, and her face, though old, is covered in scabs and acne. The absence of two front teeth complete the picture for me. Plus her aura is the color of poop. That's just how you can tell. Her arms have burn marks but no track marks, so I am guessing it is crack. She smiles at me.

"Hey, do you think we should stay in line, or just try tomorrow"?

"This is my first time, I don't know," I answer.

"Not mine. This line gives you a number, then you have to wait for your number to be called so you can get an appointment. The appointment is for any time between 9am and 4pm the next day. And if your number doesn't get called, they send you home after a whole day, and your number is no good the next day; you have to start over from scratch."

"That's fucked."

"Yeah. I'm Bridget. Wanna go get high"?

"Ethan. I don't smoke crack."

"I do. But really I'll do anything I can get my hands on, Ethan" she says. She tongues her lascivious gumhole and caresses my arm. "What do you do"?

I think fast, "Men."

Her hand drops away. "That's cool, I mean this is San Francisco. Don't you get high"?

I realize she may be under the mistaken impression I have money in my pocket.

I shrug, "I can't afford drugs. I'm already on a bunch of

anti-psychotics anyway, and they suck."

Her attention wanes, and she mutters "hold my spot," then wanders out of line, approaching the guy with the face tattoos. I don't turn around, but I can hear him shout, "get the fuck off me, whore"! Whatever manners his mother may have taught him, they were lost forever in prison.

The line has turned the corner and I can see the Welfare building now. Bridget drifts back.

"We'll know soon. The lady will come out and tell us where the cutoff is at 11:00."

As expected, a downtrodden social worker with a smudged lemon yellow polyester pantsuit comes out of the brick building holding a ping pong paddle. She stops about ten people ahead of us in line and raises her ping pong paddle.

"Listen up! If you are behind this spot in line, you won't receive a number today! Come back tomorrow"!

Bridget reasons, "Hey, at least we know we're fucked. I feel bad for the folks ahead of us who think they get a number and it's all good."

I try again the next morning, setting my alarm extra early, and arriving in line at 7:00 AM. Outside the locked gate there are maybe 150 people in front of me, good. The people in the front of the line are a better crowd than the back-of-the-line losers from yesterday. There are baby strollers, clean cut Mexican laborers, black folks who must have been looking for a job and this is all they can do in the meantime. They won't need this money for very long. There are a couple of jailbirds, and some tweakers who were awake all night but remembered to check the clock. All in all, a better crowd.

A line facing us, stretching east towards Tenth Street, forms by 8:30 am. I realize these are the people who waited in the line, got a number, got called, and were given an appointment. They are in the home stretch. When the gates open at 9:00 am, they go in first. I see now why there is a cut-off; the whole group looks to be about 200 people.

Once the 200 are all inside, they pull back the chain on our line. People shove and jump the line. There are two security guards on duty who apprehend shovers and line jumpers to escort them to the back of the line. A third security officer uses a bullhorn: "Proceed in an orderly fashion to the entrance. Do not push or shove. Do not jump the line. This is not a Who Concert, ladies and gentlemen."

There is a staticky loudspeaker, crackling with mispronounced names, presumably those of the folks who have an appointment.

The line snakes past a series of chain dividers ending at a desk manned by a very unhappy looking black lady. She has a Bates stamper, a clipboard, and a stack of blue index cards cut into four equal slips. One by one, she stamps the clipboard, then copies the sequential number onto a slip in slow, curling strokes. She asks the applicant for their name and ID. She hand writes some additional information culled from the ID next to the number on the clipboard. She holds the slip near her face while she gives her disclaimer, "This is your number. It is not a guarantee you will receive an appointment. The number is good today and today only. Do you understand"? She won't hand it to the person until they answer her. She hands them the slip, and they proceed to a giant waiting room filled with uncomfortable orange metal chairs.

After the first thirty people are served, a security guard peels off the top piece of paper from the clipboard. He walks 15 feet to a glass security window, like you see at a bank. He delivers the stamped paper under the window to a young woman protected by the glass. Within a minute or so, a different muffled loudspeaker calls out a number, and the first applicant from the line approaches the glass window with the young woman. They shout information back and forth through the bulletproof glass, then the young woman presents the applicant with a blue index card.

At intervals, the loudspeaker with the names and the loudspeaker with the numbers broadcast at the same time. Neither the name nor the number is audible in the ensuing cacophony. Then, like a rowdy crowd at a movie theater where the film has broken, the people in the waiting area howl, whistle and shout. This boorish protest works, and the number, then the name, are called in sequence.

After several hours in line, I reach the very unhappy looking black lady with a Bates stamp.

“ID"?

I take out my red velcro Madonna wallet and extract my California Driver’s License. She takes it from me in a swift, hostile motion as if to say, “What’s a white boy with a driver’s license doing at the welfare office"? She transcribes the Bates number from the clipboard to my blue slip of paper, then copies my license number and name to the clipboard. She moved like a sea tortoise on land. The process takes about five minutes. She holds my slip and repeats her disclaimer: the number is not a guarantee I will get an appointment. I nod and say , “Yes, Ma’am.” and she hands me my number: “301435.”

The loudspeaker reads out the next number “301378.” Great, I’ll be here a while. Then the loudspeaker comes to life with a recorded announcement. “The time is twelve noon. The San Francisco General Assistance office is closed between the hours of 12 noon and 1:30 pm. Please come back at 1:30 pm with your number or appointment slip to be readmitted.”

I have just enough time to run back to Northeast Lodge and make myself a sandwich. When I return to GA at 1:15, the line stretching East for people with numbers or appointments is longer than the initial line for numbers was. But when 1:30 rolls around, we all head into the waiting room with very little pushing or discord.

Keeping to myself, I pretend to be studying something

in my wallet with great intensity for a long time. I wish they had a book for me to read. There are no newspapers, no magazines, nothing. Closing time draws near, and I'm afraid my number will not make the cut-off. Then I hear my number crackle on the loudspeaker.

I head over to the bulletproof window, push my blue slip under the glass. The young woman inside the booth cross references the paper from the clipboard, types some information into a CRT, and a dot matrix printer comes to life. She separates the paper from the tractor holes along the side, talking to me at the same time. I try to put my ear against the glass to hear what she is saying, but she pounds the glass and mouths "Don't touch the glass"! She pushes a very official looking slip through the window, and shouts at the top of her lungs, "Read the back"! I can't hear her. She lives in Whoville.

The front of the slip has my name, Driver's License, and tomorrow's date. Just as Bridget had warned me yesterday, the back of the appointment slip indicates the appointment is for any time between 9 am and noon, or 1:30 pm to 4 pm tomorrow. I make a vow to raid the library at Northeast Lodge and grab a good book to read for tomorrow.

I choose "The Castle" by Franz Kafka. It's a bit dense for light reading, and my mind wanders as I wait for my appointment. The book's premise and setting are similar to my current existential surroundings. It makes me lose grip with reality, so I stop reading.

Besides, I need to concentrate on the loudspeaker, which seems to have blown a baffle or torn the cone. The numbers are clear, but the names become whale songs and porpoise cries. When "Meefin Loig" is called, I approach the window, as do several other applicants. It turns out it was my name, not theirs, and I am escorted through a doorway into a room filled top to bottom with social workers in cubicles.

Each social worker has an applicant by their desk, answering questions. The noise is deafening. I wind through a maze, following the security guard who seats me in front of a tall, noble looking black woman. Her neck is encircled by a chain holding her cat eye reading glasses. Her hair is in a modified bouffant. She sees me and purses her lips, prepared to dig into my situation and deny me my GA. I sit in the chair and introduce myself.

"I am Miss Stanfield," she says, declining my hand. "Why are you in my office"?

I look around the room and say, "Well, it's not really an office, right"? Never having known the drudgery of corporate America, nor the hopelessness of a government job, I didn't realize the breadth and depth of my insult to her station in life. We were off on the wrong foot.

Ignoring my critique of her office, she asked me "why are you looking for General Assistance"?

"Well, because the people at Northeast Lodge said I need---" She cut me off.

"You're at Northeast Lodge"?

"Yes."

"You know you don't have to wait in line if you're a medical waiver. Next time, if there is a next time, go to the doorway on Tenth Street and skip the main line. Now, let's get you set up."

She made a call to Northeast Lodge to confirm my particulars, scolded whoever answered for failing to tell me about the medical waiver entrance, and put the phone down, satisfied.

Miss Stanfield is a kind person, forced to deal with a lot of unpleasant people. I was a refreshing break for her. She had very little paperwork to fill out - David at Northeast Lodge would complete and mail in most of the forms. She swept through the folder she had created for me, checking off boxes, humming, and tapping her black-and-beige Chanel kitten heels. "Okay, if you will just sign here, initial here and here, and sign again on this page, we'll get you out of here and back to Miss Connie at the Northeast Lodge." She knows Connie?

"I love Connie." I tell her, as I sign

"I wouldn't doubt it. Everybody loves Connie." She smiles and extends her hand. I have passed her test. We shake. "Thank you Miss Stanfield."

She points me to the exit, which is opposite of where I came in. The exit door opens out onto Tenth street, just two blocks from Northeast Lodge.

CHAPTER 8 - PROJECTS

It's time for Deli Project, but before I can put on my Apron, David taps me on the shoulder and asks me to come to his room. In his office, he announces he has good news for me.

"Your room is ready at Conard House one week from tomorrow."

I offer no reaction.

"I had hoped you would be excited."

"What will I do there"?

"Pretty much the same as what you do here, but it will be less structured. They don't have mural project or deli project."

"Will I have to give my room"?

"Uh, yeah. That's how it works when you are transferred out."

"Can Connie come"?

"Connie works here, Ethan. Don't play dumb."

"Sorry, it's just so sudden. Where exactly is Conard House again"?

"It's a gigantic mansion on Jackson Street in Pacific Heights. The most beautiful parquet floors you have ever seen. You will love it, Ethan, I promise."

"I want to stay here."

"No, trust me, you don't. If you stay here, it's out to board and care." He puffs his thin Capri cigarette. "Board and care is no-man's land, Ethan. It's applesauce through a straw. James will probably be going to a board and care."

"Can I tell him you said so"?

David blows out a big puff of smoke and growls, "No, of course not! Why are you giving me attitude? I did you a solid favor, Ethan."

"Thanks. Can I go chop strawberries now"?

"Sure. Go chop strawberries now."

In the ground floor kitchen, Barbara is looking for me.

"Ethan, I need you to peel potatoes."

"I'm leaving. I mean, I'm getting out of Northeast Lodge."

Barbara beams, "I heard. You were accepted into Conard House. It's a beautiful place, Ethan. I know you will love it."

Everyone keeps saying so, but I am helpless and powerless; a prisoner in a Soviet gulag being transferred to a new prison.

This evening is my trip to SF General on the 47 Van Ness to get pricked with a needle full of mystery fluid (in all likelihood nothing). When I get to the 7th floor of SF General, the Schizophrenia Project is missing. There is just a big empty room. No Sally Christiansen, no doctors, just a black female security guard with hands on her hips.

"Hi," I say, "can you tell me where to find the Schizophrenia Project"?

"Ey, dis it." She has a charming Caribbean accent.

"No, I mean, where are they now"?

"Oh, dey pack up dem bags and go. Shot stay."

This is puzzling. "Did they leave any instructions behind"?

The security guard shakes her head.

I pile back onto the 47 and return to Northeast Lodge. It will take weeks for them to figure out what has happened, and by then, I'll be long gone to Conard House.

I was wrong, and Dr. Pablo Morales is on site for a consultation with me and two other Schizophrenia Project patients, ensuring we are put back on the full dose of Prolixin we were taking before the double blind study.

Back to nightly pills, hooray.

Within five minutes of my first dose I feel woozy. I stagger off to bed, praying my dreams will be better than this waking lobotomy.

CHAPTER 8 1/2 - FUCK

Who took my brain? Who fucking took my brain with an oyster fork and scooped it out? Who replaced my brain with cotton? I can't move, can only breathe if I lean forward. My lungs are full of fluid, my neck is stiff, my back hurts, my teeth are chattering, my arms are so stiff, I can't move them without help from one another.

Prolixin is evil.

It's been three days, and I still can't get my neck out of the vise to turn my head facing forward. It is too painful. The doctor isn't back until Monday, so I just have to keep taking these fucking medications and carry on as normal. Dixie says it's tardive dyskinesia. I hope not. That shit is permanent.

I can't walk, so I have to crawl around the house. Forget going outside. My arms won't move higher than my waist. I can't chop strawberries, so now I have a note from David saying I will be excused from Deli Project for the remainder of my stay at Northeast Lodge.

Funny thing, they all say I seem to be "getting better." If getting better means losing the ability to walk, sleep, use one's arms and leave the house, then I am getting better. They don't fucking have a clue how this shit feels. They should all have to try it for a week before they are allowed to prescribe it.

I can just see Dr. Pablo Morales, lying stunned on the floor staring into space, a thin trail of drool coursing down his cheek. David, my counselor who thinks more than anyone else I am getting better, would choke on the folds in his neck. They'd have to send for an ambulance. They are BARBARIANS!!

Fuck the establishment and fuck the monarchy and fuck the president and fuck the AMA. Fuck tinseltown and tin pan alley. Fuck them all and call them Sally. I fucking hate the world today, want to take my meds and drift away? Fuck no, gonna spit 'em in a paper towel and drop them in the doctor's morning oatmeal. How do you like these fuckin meds? Do you feel like shit for fucking with so many heads? Fuck the AMA, fuck the APA, Fuck the royals, fuck the air force. Fuck the white house fuck the congress. I won't be a stooge for society, taking fucking meds, dying quietly. Fuck the police, fuck jail and fuck the sheriff. Fuck these meds and fuck psychiatry. Fuck it all, Fuck it all, Fuck it all, Fuck it all.

Dr. Pablo Morales didn't like my attitude, but he did understand a stiff neck and paralyzed arms were a considerable handicap, and should not be noted in the charts as "getting better." He says we need to titrate down in stages. I asked him to take a Prolixin, and he looked at me like I had asked him to taste a spoonful of my feces. See, he knows better. Fucking prick.

He doesn't know what it's like when every tendon in your body is made out of a toxic cinnamon stick of pain. He doesn't know what it's like to only be able to draw shallow breaths. He doesn't fucking know anything.

I'm not at a normal dose yet, and my "tardive dyskinesia" is still causing me a lot of pain and discomfort. It only feels good when I'm asleep, but thanks to these fucking meds, I can't sleep now, either. Fuck the fucking AMA. Fuck the APA and fuck the big pharmaceutical companies inventing poison and call it medicine.

Punk rock makes so much sense. I am a plastic bag. I'm just a pill popping nutter in a consumer society. I'm a frozen pea. I mean nothing, do nothing, and people get rich off of the government charging my brain-freeze pills back to Medicare. I am a statistic, a figure, and I represent profit. My muscles tense and my neck tightens as the medicine continues its rampage through my system.

I thought the medication would wear off, but David's notes declaring I am "doing so much better' have caused Dr. Pablo Morales to keep me on too high a dose. He saw me this week, and was startled by the twitching and popping noises I was making.

I could overhear him argue with David, "I don't care! He's usually a total dingbat, and this medicine makes him easier to work with, Pablo."

"David, Tardive Dyskinesia can become permanent in many cases. Your failure to report it to me during the week is serious grounds for a lawsuit."

(Note to self: Sue David)

After 15 minutes of heated discussion, Pablo comes out of the office and says I can just go ahead and switch to Lithium. He writes a prescription for Lithium and leaves it by the drug dispensary. When he isn't looking, I swing past the doorway and steal the paper. I tear it into tiny shreds and flush it down the toilet. They can't pull this bullshit Total MK CIA experiment crap with me anymore. I am drug-free, baby. I am high on life.

Okay so it turns out destroying the prescription got a lot of people in hot water, but not me. I play innocent, no one thinks I can have anything to do with it. For now, I am just on a PRN of Cogentin, 1200 mg of Lithium (a natural mineral salt, they assure me) and nothing else. Ha ha. Fuck them all. A couple of the other patients at Northeast want to buy my Cogentin, but I need it. It makes the edges of the sunlight less sharp.

CHAPTER 10 - HORNBEAM

Hooray, it's moving day tomorrow. I'm on lithium now - no more antipsychotics. I will live far away from Michael G. Page in Pacific Heights (or "Specific Whites" as he likes to call it), so I make another date to visit him at the Civic Center Hotel. This time we set it for the afternoon.

I ask the attendant to ring Michael. Michael appears wearing a terry cloth bathrobe and a shower cap.

"Ethan, love, can you give me a few minutes so's Mama can get all ups"?

"Yeah, I can wait here or…"

"Perfect. I can't wait to catch up on all the lunatic gossip at the asylum."

He wiggles back out the lobby and into the elevator. "Five minutes, I swear."

In about 30 minutes, Michael comes down. He's wearing dark grey acid washed jeans with a black pleather overcoat and a green felt hat with a pink feather. He did his lips in black lipstick and there is a star of David drawn right where his third eye should be."

"I know it's not Yom Kippur, but I just feel so festive with it."

He has a bike messenger bag thrown over his shoulder.

"We're going shopping at Rainbow Grocery." He leads the way.

Rainbow Grocery is at the corner of 14th and South Van Ness in a warehouse. It's tiny inside, like a Gem Spa in New York, but with all organic produce, vitamins, bulk beans and folk remedies.

Michael holds the door for me and says, "I have such a major crush on the Flower Essences boy, I hope he's here."

We graze past the groceries towards the Bach Flower Essences. The guy behind the counter is not my type, but Michael blushes and takes a sharp right turn towards the Gem Elixir lady. "I can't do it"!

"What's wrong? He'll like you, just talk to him."

Michael snaps, "Easy for you to say, Ethan, you're pretty and you have a full head of hair. That boy will judge me from my leather cap to my holey boots."

I peek over the Dr. Bronner's bath soaps for a better look, and Michael pulls me by my hair two shelves lower where he can whisper right in my face.

"He'll see you"!

"It's okay, I don't have a crush on him."

"SHHHHHH"! Michael is dead serious.

"Uh, look, Michael, why don't you ask him if he can recommend a flower essence to overcome shyness. Your bashfulness seems to be the problem here."

Michael grabs my face and kisses it in several odd places. "Ethan, you are a genius." He straightens up, brushes imaginary cobwebs from his pleather jacket, and strides towards the Flower Essences aisle. He looks back towards me with sheer terror painted across his face, made all the more absurd by the Star of David bindi blighting his browline.

I shoo him to finish what he started. He frowns, but continues towards the dull dude behind the flower essences counter.

"Um, hi. I umm." He cackles and snorts, a clown on acid.

"Hey man, what's up"? The dude is super mellow. This will be easy.

"Can you tell me which flower essence helps with shyness, please"?

"Certainly. You can try some Hornbeam, maybe Wild Oats, and Centaury is always good to pack your swagger." He smiles at Michael.

"My god. It's too many choices. If you had to pick just one…"

"Hornbeam."

"Do you have a tester for a sample"?

"No, man, but I'll make you one if you like. Hold up."

I walk over to Michael while the dude turns and puts a few drops of hornbeam into a paper cup of distilled water.

"See, Michael. I told you. Easy as pie."

Michael frowns and swats me hard below the counter. The dude turns around, and Michael turns his frown upside down.

"Here you go. Have you had anything in your mouth in the past 2 hours"?

"I brushed my teeth with Ayurvedic toothpaste."

"Well," he instructs, "you might want to wait about 2 hours before taking this.

"I'll risk it."

"It should work - how long ago did you brush"?

"About 45 minutes ago."

"Yeah, why don't you do your shopping and come see me when you're done."

"Okay." Michael slouches and heads back towards the organic fruits. He bitches about organic sprouts.

"They call this shit organic, but they clean the trays with bleach, so how can it be organic, really? I mean, bleach lasts forever."

"You are right."

"After this, we're going to Tree's for vegan lunch. Have you been there"?

"Oh yeah. I love Tree's Place."

Michael makes a few more rounds and counts his pennies. The hornbeam will cost $6.00.

"Do you realize $6.00 is more than 1% of my monthly income? This shit had better work."

Michael is lucky because he gets SSI. It pays $535.00 a month, unlike GA, which only pays $120 every two weeks. Either way, I have to give all but fifteen dollars to Northeast Lodge, so it's not like it matters to me. But Miss Page is on a tight budget, so I can relate.

Before we check out of the register, Michael goes back to his homely dude and asks for the cup.

"Sure, Man. Drink up."

Michael drinks it and smiles at the dude. "You sure are cute."

"Thanks, man." The dude absorbed the compliment like he was a miracle sponge. Not a drop left to give back to Michael.

"Well, it does work," Michael gives his clown laugh again. "Sold!"

"Right on. Shall I wrap it up"?

"Yes, let's wrap it up, shall we"? Michael doesn't seem interested in the dude anymore, and the dude has never shown interest in him. But I guess the hornbeam had its effect, because Michael is unfazed.

"This," he says to me, "is going to come in handy at the Crud."

"The Crud? Oh, the Stud"! I laugh. The guy behind the counter laughs too, but it's too late for him to join our party now. We are all done.

Michael pays for everything in his handbasket and transfers it all to his bike messenger bag. We stroll down South Van Ness towards Tree's place.

"Since we're going past Safeway, I need about six bucks

worth of beans and rice," he says, "But I can't pay for it, so if you don't want to be involved, stay outside."

The old Safeway on South Van Ness near 20th is a dilapidated urine-scented grocery store. The clerks are surly and the atmosphere is unholy.

"I always do all my shoplifting here," he says, "because they are a huge corporation and they can handle the loss. I give Rainbow Grocery my money, not Safeway. Plus the people here are such pieces of shit."

I wait outside and when Michael comes out, his bike bag looks a bit heavier.

Tree's place is a vegan commune in the badlands of the Outer Mission. They operate a soup kitchen one day a week. Its official name is "The Cauliflower Collective," but since it is run by a genius named "Tree" the other name has always stuck. The collective members make a very special day out of it, every time. The men dress in drag and the women put on way too much makeup. Instead of making everybody wait in a cafeteria line, the members are waiters and waitresses who bring food to the table for the hungry masses. They make delicious vegan food to serve the indigent and others like Michael and me. The food is not just your typical vegan fare. They spend all week researching the menu. It's their duty to make vegan food taste better than the swill at a typical soup kitchen. Their mission is to guide wayward souls towards the joys of veganism.

To accompany the well researched menu, they have live music and exotic themes. Today, according to the the menu, we will be eating Dixieland Voodoo vegan.

The soy milk hush puppies taste just like their buttermilk counterparts. It comes with a Nayonnaise (soy mayonnaise) remoulade spiced with garlic and red chilis.

The main course is next. The tangy slaw is made of red cabbage, apple cider vinegar, olive oil and celery seeds. The Tofu Po'Boys served on homemade rolls taste like you're being hugged. The collective members serve us bedecked in silken florals and peacock feathers. To complete the free lunch atmosphere, the more musical of the crew serenade us with trumpets, guitars, a flute and a ukulele played by Tree himself.

The lunch date with Michael just gets better and better. He gives me a shot of hornbeam water. Fifteen minutes later, I am good friends with the supper crowd. Michael spends an inordinate amount of time chatting with the flautist named Rem. I hope there will be a love connection there some day. Tree gives out beads and we become a spontaneous parade on 23rd Street to celebrate an imaginary Mardi Gras in autumn.

As the stars fall and evening rises, I stand in the garden with Tree. I asked him how he became a vegan.

"Ethan, I've always been a vegan, it just took me a while to figure out how to eat this way."

"Do you miss meat?"

"No"

"What about eggs?" I ask.

"Here's how I feel about eggs. If a chicken were to fly into my garden, lay an egg, then fly off, I would consider eating it."

The image of a flying chicken is so absurd, I bust out laughing.

We leave Tree's place and take Harrison street to the Stud for some dancing. Despite Michael's forceful invitation, Rem chooses not to join us; Michael isn't disappointed in the least.

At the Stud, Debbie Deb warns us to "Lookout Weekend" and everything is in perfect harmony. I only started the lithium the day before, so it hasn't had time to ruin my life yet. Michael and I dance in our corner by the emergency exit. The new location is not as cool as the old one, but it will do. And the music tonight is on fire. Trinere wants to know "How Can We Be Wrong" and I guess

Whitney just wants to dance with somebody.

Since it's my last night at Northeast, I figure fuck it, let's go out for a long walk. The Stud is dying on a Sunday night like it always does, so Michael and I go to Powell and Market. The cable cars are vacant at this hour, so we catch a ride to Fisherman's Wharf. We wander the docks and talk about oh I don't know, everything under the sun. We are both hopped up on hornbeam, so we talk to dozens of tourists and strangers, who are thrilled to be talking to real San Franciscans.

"Ethan, what do you do in there, anyway"?

"Stupid shit. Take drugs. Chop strawberries."

"Ha! You should be chopping strawberries at Tree's Place."

"I know," I agree "but I'm moving to Pacific Heights tomorrow."

"It's still one bus ride - the 22 Fillmore - you could go."

"I'll have to see what the counselors say."

Michael grabs me by the lapel, "Girl, you need to get out of the mental health system as soon as possible. Do you see how they have you programmed to check before you do any shit at all"?

"You're right. I'm stuck right now."

"Yes, but get unstuck, please, the world needs you to do better things. I just feel it, Ethan. You're a poet. You have to protect your soul from the doctors and cops and your mother and anyone who wants to change you."

"Thank you for caring"!

He cherishes me. His words bring tears. My mother will be back in my life, and she will not be interested in protecting me like Michael is. He's my real mother.

The Cable Cars have stopped running, so we need to find a late night bus. We walk along the Marina to Fillmore to catch the 22. Michael ducks into a liquor store for a pack of drum cigarettes. Waiting at the bus stop is Betsy.

"Betsy! What are you doing here"?

She shakes her head as if to quiet me and then says, "Hey, Time Traveler, catching the 22"?

"Yeah. It's always so strange running into you. What are you up to"?

"I've been going to Artists Anonymous. It's good for my bipolar."

"So like you're powerless over your art and your life has become unmanageable"?

"Exactly"! She smiles and puffs her trademark brown More cigarette. Michael exits the liquor store.

"Betsy, here comes my friend Michael." I turn and watch him roll a cigarette before he lights up. Growing impatient, I wave him over, saying, "Michael, come here"! He takes his time. "Come here! I want you to meet someone."

"Don't get your panties in a bunch. I'm coming." He approaches us.

"Michael, this is Betsy."

"Who is Betsy"?

I turn back, and she's not there.

"Girl, that's some nasty medicine they give you."

"She was just here. She must have rolled away."

"Is she on roller skates? She must move pretty fast."

"No. Electric wheelchair. She was just here, I swear."

Or maybe she is an angel.

The bus chugs and wheezes up the Cow Hollow hill and tops off at Broadway.

"So this is your new home. You're gonna be right here in the Heights." Behind us the view of the Bay and the lights of Alcatraz are dizzying. In front of us are the lights of the Western Addition, orange and muddy. We hop off when the bus reaches Haight Street.

The Lower Haight is spooky this late at night, when only the crackheads from the Projects and the hookers are out. We catch the Haight bus back to Market and part ways at the Civic Center Hotel.

CHAPTER 11 - CHANCE ENCOUNTER

It's late afternoon when the taxi arrives. I have only a few possessions; packing my second-hand dad shirts and dirty jeans takes about three minutes. In the slow, congested cab ride to Pacific Heights, I remember what David said. My mom will be back in my life. I love her and miss her, but at the same time, there's a dark knot of apprehension in my belly, the kind which forms when I'm being yelled at or slapped in a fit of rage. My mother's dark side occupies my thoughts, drowning out the hugs, the ice cream and the trips to the beach which constitute her light side, free from shadows and hurt. The cab pulls to the curb and I hand the driver a medical voucher. Fancy ride, courtesy of the San Francisco Mental Health system.

Conard House is a magnificent three story mansion near the corner of Jackson and Fillmore. If you count the basement, it's four floors. The front doors is up a flight of stone steps. A couple of cigarette smokers mutter and cough. I ring the bell. A Janis Joplin clone answers and smiles. Her name is Janis, surprise surprise, and she has a clipboard, like everyone else in the mental health power structure. On the clipboard is a chart with my name.

"Hi Ethan, I am Janis, and I will be your intake counselor."

Oh god, I'm not ready for this right now. I just want to go to sleep.

"We need to ask you some assessment questions to determine if you are ready to be in a halfway house. Come on in to the office." This is different from Northeast Lodge. The counselors all share a big room. The door is wide open, and we can just walk in there. The parquet floors are even more beautiful than David had let on.

I brace myself for difficult, prying questions, but they turn out to be the same kinds of questions I had to answer to apply for SSI: Can I shave myself? Can I wake myself in the morning? ("Yes, with difficulty" to both.)

In a few minutes there will be a meeting in the common room where I have to introduce myself to the house. I want another shower, but there's no time. I sit on the sofa and wait for the clients to filter in from their rooms, their day treatment and their day jobs. The living room is empty.

Then the whole room is shaking as a muscular young man appears. His eyes are the color of Sicilian olives, his skin is well-tanned, and he wears a big grin on his chiseled face. He extends a meaty hand and introduces himself.

"Hey buddy, I'm Chance."

"Ethan." When we touch an electric pulse of sexual energy travels between us.

"Did you feel that, Ethan? What was it"? He smiles, and I am embarrassed. I am struck dumb, staring into the face of a God. He sits beside me and wraps his arm around my neck. The embrace is the kind that says, "You are my property."

"I can tell you and me we're gonna get along just fine. You're my roommate, you know." I didn't know. I am getting high from his sexual energy. This is how I felt when I had horrible crushes on straight boys in high school. I notice he wears a plain silver ring.

“Is that your wedding ring”?

He glances at his hand and grins - “It’s just a ring. Wedding rings go on the left. But I used to be married.”

I’m nervous if anyone else walks in the room they will sense our smoldering sexual energy, so I bow my head, willing it to go away. When I open my eyes, Chance is still right there and the fire is still burning. I hear the sounds of violins playing, but the stereo is turned off. Every Motown love ballad makes sense. What screwball comedy of errors has landed me next to Chance, with his arm around my shoulder? He’s straight, has an ex-wife, and now he will be my roommate. A recipe for torture.

“Ethan, little buddy, I try to skip these house meetings if I can. They think I work late hours and I don’t want to lead them to believe otherwise. I’ll be upstairs in my-- our room. Knock on the door before you come in.” He gives a serious, mischievous smile meaning ‘...because I don’t want you to catch me doing anything indecent.’ Chance sneaks out the back stairwell as the first clients make their way in.

Snapping out of my reverie, I see a cross-eyed red-head standing before me, “Hi I’m Kathleen. What’s your name"?

“Ethan”

“Ethan is Hebrew for strong. Are you strong"?

Kathleen sits beside me on the couch without hesitation., making a tight sandwich. Kathleen is a piece of bread, I’m the lunchmeat and a somber, silent woman with a blank face and greasy hair is the other piece of bread on this loveseat. A kind looking Chinese man with coke bottle glasses shuffles into the common room with two Asian ladies in tow. He lights up when he sees me. “Hi you new, right? I’m Tony. Tony Ha.” He gestures to his entourage. “This Annie, and this Mei.” I stand and shake hands with Tony. He gives off a friendly vibe.

“Ethan,” I offer. Annie and Mei don’t respond when I extend my hand to them. Tony shakes his head and whispers, "they are shy." A few moments later, a massive Chinese bull dyke walks in and slaps Tony on the back.

"Who's the new guy"? She speaks perfect San Francisco English. She must have been born here, unlike Tony, Annie and Mei.

"Bernadette, this Ethan."

"Ethan! Glad to have another one of us in here if you know what I mean." She winks as she vigorously shakes my hand. How did she know I am gay? I guess the same way I knew she was a lesbian. We just know. There's a shared sadness and fear in our eyes we cannot hide.

Tony asks me if I play Mah Jong.

"I don't, but I'm always willing to learn."

"Great! We play every night right here - this room. You join us any time. I will teach you can play real good." His English is easy to understand, bad grammar and all.

"I would like that." I squeeze my way back into my sandwich between the perma-smile Kathleen and the blank-faced piece of bread. The common room fills to standing room only.

I am uncomfortable sitting wedged between Kathleen and the vacant stare of the woman on my right. To lighten the mood, I offer my hand to Blankface and say, "Hi, I'm Ethan."

At first she doesn't respond. Her face is frozen in a waxen expression, betraying no emotion of any kind. No anger, no warmth. But then one corner of her mouth lifts a fraction of an inch into a lopsided smirkish smile. "Hi, I'm Vicki." We shake. But then her mouth returns to a neutral frown. She drops my hand like a spoiled peach. She stares straight ahead, vacant as an abandoned motel.

The four counselors toting clipboards enter the common area, and a hippy dude calls roll.

The object of the meeting is to pore over the circulars from Safeway and pick out meals we can make with the items on sale. Then once we have our shopping lists, the shopping committee will buy the ingredients. Kathleen and I form a cooking team with Vicki and some other zombies for Wednesday night's dinner. I wanted to see if Tony and Bernadette would join us, but Kathleen set me straight. "The Chinese cook together and it's really good. Same with the black people and the Filipinos. I like Chinese best."

"What about the Mexicans"?

"There aren't that many right now. Some of them are Salvadoran and they won't cook with the Mexicans anyway. Too many arguments."

Hamburger is on sale, as is sweet Italian sausage. Kathleen says we should make spaghetti with sausage and meatballs. I don't argue - she is experienced at this, and I am happy to let her lead the way. We build our shopping list, which includes breadcrumbs, salad and the fixings for Garlic Bread - enough for the 22 residents of the halfway house. I forgot meatballs are made with breadcrumbs, but Kathleen has the whole recipe in her head.

"My mother is half Irish half Sicilian, and my Dad is Scottish and Roman, so I learned how to cook Italian. What about you, Ethan? What's your background"?

"Scottish and Jewish." Kathleen perks up when I say "Scottish."

"Ta brae nacht na bricht"!! she shouts. "It's a fine night tonight, in Scottish Gaelic." Kathleen is studying Irish Gaelic on her own free time, and she has learned a few expressions in Scottish Gaelic, which is different from Irish but has similar words. "Camar ha," she says, "is how you say hello. And Slainte means 'cheers.'"

Kathleen's mind is a storehouse of obscure and eccentric knowledge. If it were a living room, it would need to be vacuumed.

The meeting is over and all the shopping lists have been turned in. Janis removes my bag from lockup and walks me two flights to my room. "Number 6 at the end of the hall. I gotta get back downstairs for activity report. You can join next time." and she leaves.

I knock, as Chance had asked; I don't hear anything. I poke my head into the space. The room is an attic space on the third floor with two small single beds. I drop my backpack at the foot of my bed and put items into my dresser while Chance rolls over in his bed and just stares at me, grinning and rubbing his hands along his legs…a probable side effect of the medication. I have to clear things up,

"Chance, are you gay"?

"Who me? Not really. I'm bi."

"Well if your gay part of you was in charge, would you like me"?

"What do you think, Ethan"?

"I think you're straight. I don't think you like me."

He looks a bit perplexed. "Well, we only just met. I hope you didn't get the wrong idea there when I put my arm around you."

"N-n-no," I stammer, "We're sharing a room, so it's good to lay all our cards on the table, right"?

"This is an awkward and unnecessary conversation, Ethan."

"Sorry I brought it up."

Chance rolls away so his back is to me and he says, "Don't be." And he leaves it all mysterious. Fuck I hate that. Don't be...what the hell does he mean?

I don't want to go to sleep without knowing more about him.

"So Chance, you said you work late. What do you do?"

Chance rolls back to face me. "I said they think I work late hours. I don't. But I do work, early. I fix Vespas."

"I have wanted a Vespa ever since I saw Diva."

"That was a Motobécane Mobylette. I'll bet you mean Quadrophenia."

"Yeah, you're right. I just know I want one. A friend of

mine had one and he used to drive me around Berkeley. It was the coolest bike ever."

"Lambrettas are even cooler."

"What kind of bike do you have"?

Chance frowns. "I don't. I lost pretty much everything when I got hospitalized. But I'll buy a Lambretta when I've saved enough."

"When you do, you're taking me for a ride on the Great Highway." I don't know where the Great Highway came from, it just popped into my head. A romantic vision.

"Deal."

Neither of us asks about what got us into the hospital. It's just one of those things you don't do in the Mental Health system. I'll bet Chance has a story even better than mine.

CHAPTER 12 - OBLIGATIONS

Chance works a full time job, so he is already out of the room when I wake and shuffle to breakfast. He isn't at breakfast either, so he must have left for work.

The awesome part of being in a halfway house-- you are surrounded by people who have reached a higher level of functioning. Many of us are getting better. Some of us are staying the same, but we are functioning. The reverse side of this coin is how they expect more from us. At Northeast Lodge, you just had to go on coffee walk once a week to satisfy the activity requirements. At Conard House, you have to do three activities a week, and coffee walk only counts as one. At breakfast, Kathleen clues me in on how to get away with the bare minimum.

"If you go to Safeway on Saturday and do the grocery shopping, it counts as one activity; if you sign up for a cleaning chore around the house, it also counts as an activity. Then all you need is coffee walk, and you're set."

Great, but they expect you to do an all day activity during the week, like Chance who works, or Kathleen, who goes to day treatment.

Janis is my counselor, and she is tasked with assigning me to a full time daytime activity. If I could, I would choose "sleep all day" as my activity but it isn't an option. I would rather be lobotomized than return to day treatment. Janis says I can volunteer somewhere if I want. "It's a great way to gain new skills for employment when you're ready to return to the work force." Her words fall like raindrops on turtle wax. Considering how shaving and putting my pants on right way forward are major challenges for me, I distrust I can find a job requiring my set of zero skills. I do need money. With money, I can buy my way out of here. I know it would be good for my soul to volunteer at Tree's house. I know. But not having money is terrifying.

"Janis, if I can find a paying job wouldn't that count"?

"Of course, Ethan. You might want to start with volunteer work first, just to get your feet wet before jumping back into the workforce."

"But there are lots of people living here who work, right"?

"Sure. Vicki works at the post office."

"Vicki has a job? She can't even smile"!

"Ethan, it's a disability, and the post office can accommodate her illness. She is a mail sorter. It's the same job she has had for twenty-five years."

Janis has a point; you don't need much personality to sort mail.

"How long do I have to choose my daytime activity"?

"Well," Janis strokes imaginary chin hairs, "technically you need to decide today. But I can give you until the beginning of next week. Will it be enough time"?

It isn't, but I say, "Yes. It's perfect."

"And as for your three extra-curricular activities…"

"I'll do the shopping, a chore, and coffee walk."

Janis is disappointed with me."You know, we have movie night at the Kabuki, sometimes we get free seats at the ballet and even nosebleed seats at the opera, so you may want to mix it up a bit. You choose your activities each week, so if you decide you want to go see a movie, just switch it up."

"Do you ever get Madonna tickets"?

"Not unless she plays Symphony Hall."

Madonna plays the Cow Palace, not the Symphony. Oh well. "What about clubbing? Can I go to Das Klub as one of my activities"?

"No, they serve alcohol. And no, you can't go on coffee walk twice, just in case it was your next question."

It wasn't, but I nod and look disappointed.

"Your chore this week is to straighten the library. It can double as your daytime activity while you get yourself situated."

"Sounds great." It sounds like torture, but it's easy and I don't have to think about it much.

Dinner is lackluster, but home cooked. The best part of the meal is the Pillsbury biscuits. The chuck steak is full of gristle, and the oven baked fries taste like creosote. I look for Chance, but he is nowhere to be found. His job must pay well, so he eats out often.

After dinner, I wind my way to the basement living room, where the TV is tuned to the news, followed by Magnum, P.I. Tom Selleck is supposed to be handsome, but I don't see it. He looks gay with his thick mustache. Wouldn't it be funny if Tom Selleck the ladies man were gay?

"Ethan"! I hear Kathleen call from the top of the stairs.

"What"? I shout back.

"Phone call. She says she's your mother."

A profound dread washes over me. My skin prickles and burns.

At the landing at the top of the stairs is a payphone. Kathleen is talking into the receiver. "Camar ha means hello in Scottish, and ta brae nacht…" she trails off mid-sentence and hands the phone to me.

"Mom"?

"What the fuck took you so long? Who was that crazy bitch"?

"Kathleen isn't a bitch. I was downstairs watching Tom Selleck."

"I hate his mustache," she says. "Look, I got a place in the city and I want to give you my number. Do you have a pen and paper"?

"No, but hold on." I drop the phone and wander off in search of writing utensils. The door to the counseling office is open a crack, so I peek in. Gwyneth, the night counselor, sees me.

"Can I help you"?

"Yeah, I need a pen and paper."

"Sorry, we can't give those out. House rules. You can go to Walgreens on California Street."

"My mom needs to give me her number and she's on the phone."

Gwyneth sees my panicked expression and takes pity. She hands me a post-it note and one of those stubby pencils they use at the bowling alley or golf course. "I need you to return the pencil immediately."

"Thank you." What a strange economy exists in the mental health system. Pencils trade like junk bonds.

I return to the pay phone, and the receiver is back on the hook. Some misguided Samaritan hung up on my mom. Of course the phone rings within seconds, and I answer.

"Hello"?

"Ethan, what the fuck is going on over there? Did you hang up on me"?

I roll my eyes and take a deep breath before answering. "I don't know, I was only away for a minute getting something to write your number and when I came back, the phone was hung up."

"Yeah, well when I called back, whoever answered said you had gone to bed. Are you shining me on? Really, what kind of bullshit are you pulling here"?

"Mom, it's a weird place, okay? There are crazy people here. I can't fucking help it if you had a bad customer experience on the fucking pay phone."

Her voice takes on the screechy tone that hurts my ears. "Watch your filthy mouth! Don't talk to me like that"!

"Can I just have the number"? I'm too tired to argue she started our conversation by swearing at me. In her world, she's beyond reproach. If I call her on it, she denies it ever happened. Sometimes I wonder if she's like Sybil with multiple personalities who don't remember what the other one is doing.

"Yeah, okay it's 415-286-3299. Did you get it"?

"415-286-3299. Got it. Where do you live now"?

"It's this cool apartment in the Mission District. You should come visit. Are you busy tomorrow"?

"I have to organize the library and then a 3pm meeting. Maybe we can have dinner"?

"Sure. Dinner would be fine. Shall I cook"?

I hate her cooking, which she knows. There is only one correct answer to this trick question.

"Yeah. Make pork chops." I hate pork chops, but this is all part of the strategy.

"No, I think I'll make spaghetti. Is spaghetti okay"?

I try to sound disappointed, rather than relieved. "Oh, okay. Yes. It's fine, mom."

"Great. I'll pick you up at six. Wait outside for me; I don't want to have to find parking in your neighborhood. I want you outside waiting when I get there. Are we clear"?

"Crystal clear. See you at six tomorrow."

"Okay, honey, I love you."

"I love you too, mom."

In the common room, there's a loud persistent clatter. I want to go see what is causing the noise, but I am enervated. I use the last of my strength to drag my ass upstairs to room 6. Chance isn't home. It must be nice to come and go as he pleases.

In the morning, I make myself scarce and go for a visit with Michael G. Page.

"Girl, I know that look. You are sweet on somebody."

I want to deny it, but it's true. I make a feeble attempt to change the subject.

"He's not interested in me. Hey, are those new pants"?

"Bitch, you know these pants are the same filthy pants you seen me in at the Stud a hundred times. Don't try and change the subject. Who is he"?

"Uh, well he's my roommate at Conard House--"

Michael cuts me off, "No! You have to be careful with roommates!"

"So let's talk about your pants, then."

"There's nothing to talk about. I want the tea on this roommate. What's his name? What does he look like"?

"Um, he's pretty old, 35 years old or so. And he's straight."

"Not what I asked. What's his name and what does he look like"?

I sigh, "His name is Chance. He has olive skin, pale green eyes, and he says he drives a motorcycle, although come to think of it I've never seen it."

Michael leans in. We're at the counter of the Rolling Pin Donut on Castro. Two stools away from us is an old man, a legend, who always sits on the same barstool in loose white OP corduroy shorts. He lets his oversized dick and balls hang out for passersby on Castro. I figure when he's not there on the stool, he's off having sex with some size queen.

"You've never seen his bike. Do you think he's a liar? They got a lot of liars in there. And how do you know he's straight"?

I wish Michael weren't acting like Chance was a possible boyfriend. Not a chance in hell. "Well, I asked him."

"How brave," he pauses. "What was his answer"?

"Okay, okay he said he's bi."

"Oh my god girl! The bisexuals make the best fucking boyfriends. When are you making your move"?

"I don't have any moves. He's nice, end of sentence." But for some reason, I can't wipe the stupid smile off of my face.

"Ethan, I see it all over your face. You have a crush."

"Fine, fine. You got me. Chance is sex on a stick with wheels. We have not found our way into each other's arms, and I'm not his type."

"Did he actually say you're not his type"? Michael should be an interrogator.

"I don't exactly remember what he said but it was something close."

"I need it word for word."

"All right, he said something to the effect of 'We just met. I hope you didn't get the wrong idea when I put my arm around you."

Michael gasps. "He put his arm around you"?

"Yeah, but like he said, I would be getting the wrong idea if I thought he was into me."

"Nonsense. He left the door wide open. All you gotta do is walk in." Michael looks around as if a waiter might appear at the donut shop. "This coffee used to be free refills, but now they make you pay a quarter. It's outrageous! For some of us, a quarter is a lot of money."

Michael hops off the stool and asks the Asian donut man for a free refill.

"No. You pay quarter or no coffee." Michael looks at his feet and sees a shiny quarter right next to his left combat boot. He bends over picks it up, and hands it to the donut man, who seethes and refills the cup.

As Michael comes back to our window counter, he encourages the old guy with a pat on the back. "You dropped your nutsack, but hey, if you got it, flaunt it." The old man smiles, chuckles then goes back to concentrating on the school of fish swimming past the window, hoping to hook one with his prodigious worm.

"Ethan, you need to introduce me to this Chance character. I need to sniff all up in his stuff and make sure he's your future ex husband."

"He works strange hours, so it would be hard to predict if he's there."

"Come on, Ethan. Look at the top of Castro. The 24 Divisadero; it's divine providence. Do you have your crazy card and 15 cents for the bus"?

"Yes."

"Great, do you have an extra 15 cents I can borrow"?

"I got a quarter and a nickel."

"That works."

We dash across 18th Street to catch the 24 Divisadero. Michael has to smuggle his coffee onto the bus.

"Transfer, please" - the bus driver tears off a transfer for Michael. Michael inspects it. "I'm sorry sir, this transfer is only good for one hour. I think your pad might have slipped." Transfers in San Francisco employ a medieval technology. They are printed with today's date and are bordered in bright colors. On the main body of the transfer there are two columns. On the left are the numbers 1 through 12, which repeat once. On the right are the numbers 00am 30am 12 times, then 00pm 30pm another 12 times. To set the expiration on the transfer, the driver has to slide and skew the pad of transfers at an angle so when torn off, will produce a minimum 90 minutes expiration time. This gives the rider about 2 hours before the transfer expires. At the top of the transfer is a little perforated tab "Void if Detached." That's the first transfer. The second transfer is the colorful transfer. There is no third transfer, but most bus drivers will let you keep the second transfer. Michael needs more time if he plans to hang out in Pacific Heights for more than a minute. The bus driver adjusts the pad of transfers to allow 2 hours and 30 minutes for Michael.

The 24 Divisadero is a clunky electric bus traveling through the Castro, across the Western Addition, then rises to Jackson Street, where it's just a short walk to Conard House. When it crosses Haight street, there is a 40% chance the trolley poles will come unjoined from the overhead cables, and the driver will have to step off the bus at great peril and reattach them to the wires. This is what happens when things are not going well. I have a growing sense of dread. Chance and Michael are from two different worlds. I don't think it will be a pleasant meeting, if it even happens.

We disembark at Divisadero and Jackson. Michael rolls me a Drum and lights it before he rolls his own. He's a sweet man under his dark, angular exterior. We walk in silence, refueling our nicotine cells.

At Conard House, there are a few clients hanging out on the steps. I don't know them very well except for Bill, a schizophrenic garbage man. "Hey Bill, do you know if Chance is here"?

Bill shrugs, takes a long drag off of his cigarette, and says "Nope. No Chance."

I am relieved. "Oh well, I guess it wasn't meant to be."

I wait with Michael for 35 minutes before an overstuffed 22 Fillmore stops at Jackson. A couple of people get off, so Michael figures he can fit. I wave as he wedges himself into the mass of humanity. He blows a kiss as the bus pulls out, shudders then wheezes down the hill.

Today I have to clean the Conard House library. The "library" is a dusty room in the basement filled with bookshelves and a jumble of paperback books, comic books, and records. They are muddled and snarled, like what you would expect to find at a mismanaged thrift store. With no one to help me, this is one of the labors of Hercules.

I return upstairs to ask Janis if she has something else for me.

"I can't do this by myself, it's too much."

Janis gets a twinkle in her eye. It is both frightening and intriguing

"Ethan, this won't be a one hour walk in the park. Think of it as a marathon, spread out over several days. Start by telling me what you mean by 'too much.'"

I consider the question, "I need help."

"That's not what I asked. What do you mean by too much"?

"There's over two thousand books, 500 comic books, and I don't know how many records down there. Do we even have a record player"?

"We do, in the common room. It's not like we can afford a CD player."

"Now you mention it, I did see a record player in there."

"Back to the question about this being 'too much.' Ethan, can you envision yourself alphabetizing 20 books"?

I scoff, "There's 2,000"!

"Again, not what I asked. Can you picture yourself picking 20 books from the pile and putting them in alphabetical order"?

"It won't work because I'll spend the whole time putting books in between other books."

"You're jumping ahead a bit, but good thinking. How would you organize this, if it wasn't too much"?

Damn, she's good. I gotta hand it to her. "I would pre-sort by type, so comic books, books, and records were in their own piles, then pick the smallest pile first."

"You have the beginnings of a good plan, Ethan. What would be the next step"?

"I would have to see how many shelves worth of stuff I have, and then assign those shelves for the records, which are the smallest pile."

Janis asks, "Do you have to finish by our house meeting at 3pm"?

"No, I don't. I have all week to finish, right"?

"You have months to get it done if you want. But I don't recommend it. Today, do what you can and then we'll see if you need help."

The light in the basement library is a 25-watt bulb, which contributes to the gloomy sense of dread, but I have a plan now. A good plan. I find three empty corners and use them for the pre-sort. Like a gleaner in a garbage pile, I pick out the records and stack them in the first corner. This music is stale. No 12-inch singles in this group. Paul Mauriat, Engelbert Humperdinck, Henry Mancini, Ogden Nash, Allan Sherman - these are grandma records.

Seeing these records reminds me of the job I had in New York City. For five dollars an hour under the table, I worked at Second Coming Records. I had a prestigious cashier gig in the rock store, until I dyed my hair pink. Andre and Gladys, the world's meanest people and owners of the store, told me I looked like a "fucking fairy" and banished me to the soundtracks, show-tunes and vocals store across the street. Some of the coolest gay people in the city shopped there, but I was embarrassed and angry because I wasn't allowed to work in the rock store. I was supposed to play vocal music from the store collection, but I wanted to play Led Zeppelin and David Bowie like we played across the street. So instead it was Paul Mauriat because the cover looked cool, and the Village Stompers because I thought they might be punk rock. I was indignant. I didn't even care when Fred Schneider came in and bought an Yma Sumac album, nor when Mark Almond bought the original Broadway cast of Hair. One day I played a Doris Day 45 single on endless repeat until customers complained. My secret love was no secret anymore.

But such a memory stretches across a giant chasm with a big ugly hospital in the middle. Nothing is the same now. I have about a hundred records stacked in the corner, and the rest are buried out of sight under comics and regular books. The comics don't weigh very much, so I move on to them.

Superman, Archie, Richie Rich, Wendy the Witch, Casper the Ghost...this is not worthy of a library. There's some cultish comic called "Teenage Mutant Ninja Turtles." It's not as cool as it sounds. No R. Crumb, no Frank Miller. I dump armfuls of comics into the opposite corner and glean a few more exposed records from the pile. I even find "Let it Bleed" by the Stones. I wish the record player were here. It would make the work go by quicker. I lost my Walkman when I got arrested, so I can't listen to tapes.

What remains is a big pile of books.

Records will be easy - alphabetical by artist or composer, V for Various - just like we did at Second Coming.

Comic books - I think alphabetical by character will work.

As for books, fiction will be alphabetical by author, and nonfiction...hmmm. Alphabetical by topic might work, but it might not. Sometimes it's hard to pinpoint the topic. Like this book "The Magic of Findhorn" - would it go under G for gardening, P for plants, R for religion or S for Spirituality? Or this book, "Let's Go The Budget Guide to Mexico 1986" - M for Mexico or T for travel? Wait, this book is cool. I'm borrowing it.

Let's Go The Budget Guide to Mexico 1986 is published by the Harvard Student Agencies, which, if I'm not mistaken, means real Harvard students write the book. The cover boasts "revised and updated every year." So this book is last year's model. How much can change in a year? I can't wait to find out back in the room, but for now, I need to concentrate on sorting library books.

I'm debating about whether to separate hardcover books from the paperbacks, but it wouldn't make sense. If you're reading a book, who cares whether it's hardback or paperback? Bookstores separate them because the hardcovers are worth more. But this is a library for mentally ill people, and no one cares whether the book is worth a penny or a hundred dollars. They just want to read. So I scratch the separation plan.

It occurs to me this would be a good time to go see Janis and ask for some guidance, but I think she'll just use the Socratic method and I'll have to make the decision myself anyway. So hmmmm…fiction and nonfiction are two different kingdoms – plant and animal, so they will have to be the top-level sort.

Fiction will be easier, because I can alphabetize by author. It could be divided into mysteries, fantasy and science fiction, literature…but this is Conard House, not A Clean Well Lighted Place for Books, so screw it. I'll cross the Nonfiction bridge when I get to it. I should pop over to Van Ness and see how they sort nonfiction at A Clean Well Lighted Place for Books. Part of my "activity." right? I'll have to get Janis to agree. She will think I'm scamming her, but I need to know the best way to handle non-fiction…I'm getting ahead of myself and I need to stay focused.

My experience at Second Coming paid off, and I had the entire collection of over 300 records sorted and alphabetized on a bookshelf just in time for our 3pm meeting in the common room.

I'm not early this time, so I have to stand. Tony Ha offers his seat to Vicki, who looks like she needs it. He stands next to me.

"Ethan, we missed you at Mah Jongg last night."

"Yeah, sorry. My mom called, and then I had to go to sleep."

"When she call, I tell her you asleep. She mean, mean lady."

"Yeah, she mean, mean lady alright." Tony Ha is a wise man.

After the meeting, I still have two and a half hours until

my mother arrives. Sally Jessy Raphael is a crashing bore, and the news gives me anxiety, so I opt out of TV. I remember the Let's Go Mexico book I set aside, and bring it to the room.

Chance is hiding out, avoiding the meeting. He sees the book and grows curious.

"What you got there"?

"A travel guide to Mexico. I'll read it and pretend I'm going."

"Why don't you go for real"?

I laugh and say, "yeah, right"!

"No, really, dude. The peso keeps falling. You could spend a month there for a hundred dollars easy."

"According to this book, I say, referring to the exchange rate in the front, the peso is 400 to the dollar. A nice hotel room costs 24,000 pesos, so it would be sixty dollars right there."

"First of all, you don't need a nice hotel room. Second, the peso fell over 1,000 to the dollar. It's at 1,600 right now."

I perk up. "Really"?

"Yeah man, it was on the news last night. Weren't you paying attention? They're having a crisis. It's a perfect time to go. The same hotel room would cost less than 30 bucks. And if you rough it, you can stay in a clean motel for two bucks."

"I don't know, I've never been out of the country. Don't I need a passport"?

"Not for Mexico. Read the book. Man, I kinda want to go with you."

"You want to go with me"? My heart hurts. Nature plays cruel tricks on us. We ache to be with someone and they want to be with us, but not the same way. The Smiths said it best, "I Want The One I Can't Have."

"Yeah, Ethan. It would be cool."

I bury my nose in the book, learning about planes, trains

and automobiles, money, traveler's checks, bus routes, cities and ruins. This is fascinating. Chance is right; I should go. I turn to tell him about Palenque and freeze when I see the red LED alarm clock reads 6:07 p.m. Outside, I hear a car horn blasting.

I take the stairs two at a time, slide across the parquet entryway and out the front door. Double parked in front, blasting her horn, is my mother. Her face bears the grimace of Faye Dunaway in the famous wire hanger scene from Mommie Dearest. This won't be a fun-filled evening.

"What did I tell you!? Do you realize I almost got a ticket for double parking"?

I point to an empty parking space, "There's a spot right there, mom." I know this is not the right move to make in this chess game, but I just want to sacrifice my rook.

"You're missing the point, Ethan. When I ask you to be out front waiting, I expect you to be there. What could you possibly be doing worth making me wait half an hour for you"?

I know I should not question her hyperbole. Maybe she got here 23 minutes early. How do I get out of this? "I'm sorry. I had diarrhea."

"Oh, not your irritable bowel"? She looks concerned now.

I nod. "It still hurts a little, so could we please get on the road? I might need to use your bathroom." Bingo!

She capitulates, "I think yelling at you didn't help either, did it"?

I shrug, not wanting to disagree with her, and not wanting to make her feel bad, leading to accusations of "guilt tripping." She's out in Fillmore traffic now, passing the expensive shops where wives and mistresses buy their clothes and household goods. Now that I'm not cringing in fear, I look at her car, which is a Honda Accord hatchback. It's brand new. "Hey mom, is this a new car"?

"Yes, I got it so we can be together more often. Plus all

the jobs are on the peninsula, so I need a car if I'm going to make any money."

"Is this a new car"?

She nods, "Grandma Joan bought it for me."

Inside, my first thought is 'Wow, I wish my mother had bought me a car,' but I'm trying to keep this visit on an even keel. "How great! It's really nice. Can I turn on the radio? Hey, it has a tape player, too." I push play on the tape and I hear my mother's voice, talking to someone. She's crying. She reaches over and switches to KSAN, a country station on FM radio.

"What was the tape"?

"Well, it was something I wanted to talk to you about, but you don't need to hear it. Leslie took me to see a psychic while you were in the hospital. Not a storefront gypsy, this lady was the real deal. She's friends with Jane Roberts, the lady who channels Seth."

"She sounds good." I play along but don't let my guard down.

"Anyway, we taped the session. I was just so worried about you, and I felt so helpless because they wouldn't let me see you. So I asked her to do a remote healing for you. She used to do stuff for NASA too."

"Wow, cool." It sounded cool, despite my misgivings. The country music playing is the shitty crap with the slide guitars and boring white people singing about heterosexual drama. "May I change the station to KMEL or KRQR"?

"No, leave it on KSAN." When I was younger, KSAN was my favorite radio station. It played AOR, and on Sunday evenings it hosted the Dr. Demento show, which was the best thing to ever exist on radio. The only other AOR station was KMEL – the Camel. Then one day KSAN decided competing with KMEL was hurting their profits, so they switched to country music. This was right around the time John Travolta came out in "Urban Cowboy." Loyal KSAN fans were so pissed, a group of them rented a dump truck full of cow manure and unloaded it on the front steps of the station. It was a brilliant symbolic protest for a worthy cause.

KRQR is the closest thing we have to KROQ, a new wave station out of LA. KRQR plays a lot of British bands and calls themselves "the rock of the eighties." It is sort of played out now in 1987, but years ago, in 1983 and 1984, it was the shit. But none of it matters, because I am just sitting here listening to Merle Haggard sing about being an Okie from Muskogee, even though he was born and raised somewhere near Bakersfield. What a bunch of poseurs.

My mother's new apartment is on Linda Street, a dead end alleyway next to a park with tennis courts. There was parking right out front, which was unusual for the Mission. "I always have parking. See, the tennis courts have parking over on Valencia, and since there are only a few apartments on this street, there's fewer cars."

"You did pretty well."

"Well, wait until you see the apartment before you decide anything."

Upstairs, the apartment is nice. Her bedroom is in the front. It only has a view of the tennis courts and the spire of a few churches, including Mission Dolores, but it's a nice place. The landing at the top of the stairs is the living room. It's a narrow room or a very wide hallway, depending on your perspective. "This is where I meditate." She has her colorful Tibetan cushions arranged and a little shrine. "I was meditating four to six hours a day in Vermont, so this is a step down." She's guilt tripping me, but I refuse to take the bait. She prattles on. "The good news is the Dharmadhatu is over on Sixteenth and Mission, so it's easy to walk to temple."

"You mean by the Bart station"? Sixteenth and Mission is a craphole where the desperate and the lurid meet to transact sales of cocaine, methamphetamine and heroin. Isn't it a weird place for a Buddhist temple"?

"Not really. The meditation we do is removing the bad karma in the air there. It's not quite so simple, but that's the basic idea."

The bathroom has a clawfoot tub and a wrap around shower curtain. "Do you need to use the bathroom"? Mom looks concerned.

"Nah, my tummy feels better."

Mom leads me back to her kitchen. It's a big kitchen with a gas stove and a seventies avocado colored refrigerator.

"This is where I cook, obviously."

"Duh." I say it just right. She laughs. There's the feeling I miss. All the horrible tension and drama is worth waiting for a good laugh with my mom. I can bring out a good side of her if I work at it long enough, and it can make the other shit bearable. If we get enough laughs going, the eggshells disappear and I can walk without fear, so long as I guess what will set her off. If I guess wrong, and tell the wrong joke or bring up a topic which fills her face with venom, then the eggshells crash to the floor all around me. But for the moment, I'm enjoying what I have come to call my mother's love.

"Ethan, I almost forgot. I was telling you about the psychic session."

I don't know if I want to hear about it, but I have no choice.

"She specializes in identifying your power animal. Mine is a dolphin."

"Nice. Don't go near any tuna boats." More giggles.

"She told me your power animal is a seal, and you're trapped under the ice right now."

Whether it's reasonable or not, I feel like she violated my personal space; she went and had some psychic decide my power animal and then put it in a bad situation. I want to say something about it, but instead I say, "Huh."

Mom tries to read something into my noncommittal

grunt, but fails. "Yeah, so she's pulling some strings with the angels to get you out of there."

"That would be great. It's cold and hard to breathe down here." Playing along leads to more smiles and kind behavior, so I keep my secret seething to myself. First of all, my power animal is a Killer Whale and he eats your fucking dolphin…A drowning seal? Shark sausage? Really?

"Here, I got you this to keep with you at all times." She hands me a framed postcard of a fat arctic seal lying on its belly, looking at the camera.

"At all times, mom? Is it okay if I keep it in my room? The frame is kind of big to fit in my pocket." I'm treading on thin ice now. But she capitulates.

"You're right. I mean don't ever lose it, and keep it near your bed where you sleep."

"Sure, mom. No problem."

After dinner, looking around the apartment, I notice there's no couch. There are only the kitchen chairs to sit on.

"Where will the couch go"? I ask.

"What couch? The living room is too small for a couch with all my meditation cushions and the shrine."

She's right. I had assumed I could crash with Mom after Conard House, but unless I want to sleep in the kitchen, it doesn't look likely. I told her I could manage on my own when she went off to Vermont just before my high school graduation, so I can't complain. I wish she had been there to see me graduate. It would have felt normal.

"Hey mom, my curfew is at ten, so can we go back to Conard House now"?

"If you take Linda Street to 18th, make a left, then make a right on Guerrero. At 16th, you can catch the 22 Fillmore." She's right, but it's after dark and the Mission is pretty awful. But I have my crazy card that lets me on the bus for 15 cents. So I can save her time and gas. No sense arguing.

"Do you have 15 cents for the bus"?

"Isn't it a dollar"?

"Not for people in the mental health system. Just 15 cents." I show her my card, which is a very flattering picture of me.

"What a great picture. Let me give you some change." She fishes around in the bowl where she keeps her keys and extracts a dozen pennies, 3 nickels, a dime and a quarter.

"Thanks mom, I love you." I mean it, and she knows it.

"I love you too. Please get better soon so I can go back to my life."

"I'm trying."

On the bus ride home, I think about my troubles. I still need to plan with Janis so I have 4-5 hours of activity during the day. I could get a job like Chance has. Chance says he works at a motorcycle shop on Van Ness, repairing Italian bikes and scooters. The 22 is supposed to go up the hill past Broadway and then down into the Marina, but the bus driver pulls over at California and tells everyone to step off and wait for the next bus. He pulls the electric cable arms down, locks the bus and walks away. Off to score some drugs. I check all of Fillmore Street; there isn't a bus in sight. It's only five blocks to Jackson Street, so I might as well walk.

Between Sacramento and Clay I see a help wanted sign in the window of a coffee shop called "Sweet Inspirations." Even though it's late, they are still open and busy. They sell desserts and espresso drinks. I ask a young guy for an application but he looks at me and says we can skip the application for now; he can interview me first.

"I'm Damon. And you are…"?

"Ethan."

"Do you live nearby"?

"Yes, I live in a house on Jackson Street."

"Is it walking distance"? He isn't asking typical job interview questions.

"It's just there, yeah."

"It's part time 4 nights a week and I need someone to start tomorrow night. Can you work tomorrow night? I'll train you."

"Sure." I panic inside because I don't know if night work will sit well with Janis, but outside, I remain calm and composed. Besides, Vicki works graveyard at the post office.

Damon hands me a job application. "Okay, then, fill this out and bring it to work with you tomorrow. The shifts are Thursday through Sunday from 7pm to midnight. Any other questions"?

"How much does it pay"?

"It's minimum wage – $3.65 an hour, plus tips. It's a tip jar and we split it all evenly. So see you tomorrow at 7:00"?

"Thursday at 7:00." I leave the place feeling as if a pair of Inuit vegetarians rescued my seal from the ice, and now they plan to make me their beloved family pet.

CHAPTER 13 - MAH JONG

Janis looks skeptical when I tell her about the job, but she nods. "Ethan, it's no problem. You can work nights, as long as you cook dinner one night. Will your schedule shift around much"?

"I don't know. I don't think so. Thursday, Friday, Saturday and Sunday nights from 7pm to midnight."

"Then great. We found your activity. Are you excited"?

"Hells yeah. I wanted a job. But will it affect my GA?"

"We can talk about it in session tomorrow."

"Cool."

As I head towards the stairs, I hear the clattering sound from the common room. Curiosity gets the better of me, so I investigate.

The corner table is pulled away from the wall. Annie, Bernadette, Mei and Tony Ha are sitting around the table, swirling a bunch of giant dominoes in a whirlpool pattern. Tony sees me, and a huge grin spreads over his face.

"Ethan, you here to join us! Here! Sit! Sit! You have my place." He stands up, offering me his seat.

"I should just watch you play first." Behind me, the dominoes change from a cacophony of swirling to the gentle click, click of tiles being stacked.

"No, come come come! You sit down." He strong-arms me into his seat. The dominoes are now arranged in four walls, two dominoes high.

Tony pats me on the shoulder. "Good, Ethan, you have fun. I watch and help."

I doubt I will have fun. Fun has been off the table since the day I landed in jail. I have had a few laughs, but I feel like crap and hate everything about my life.

Annie, the shyest in the group, reaches out and turns a domino upright. It's a green Chinese symbol. The ladies at the table draw a gentle breath, look at me, and smile.

"What, what happened"?

"We play halfway house rules," says Tony. "Some people use dice but we draw tile to start. But green dragon isn't a number, so we have to draw again."

"Why did Annie smile at me, though"?

"Green dragon good luck," reasons Tony, "and Annie smile because you bring good luck, even though she lose her turn."

Mei reaches out and turns over a tile. This one has 3 small circles. Mei counts in a counterclockwise motion and reaches the third wall of tiles, in front of Bernadette. She counts three tiles in, and draws four tiles at once, turning them upright in front of her. Bernadette grabs the next four tiles, and now all eyes are on me. I collect four tiles. Annie and Mei nod. Bernadette compliments me, "Four at a time, you're a fast learner."

The circle continues four tiles at a time, and I stand my tiles in front of me. After everyone has grabbed three groups of four tiles each, Mei does something odd. She takes two tiles, the first top tile and the third top tile. Then Bernadette takes the 1st bottom tile. Tony nudges me, "You take top tile." I take the second top tile which is now the first top tile. Then Annie takes the tile underneath. These tiles are beautiful. They are much thicker than a domino, so they stand tall on their own. The backs are made of a rich brown bamboo. While I admired the tiles, the ladies have stood all of theirs upright. They arrange their tiles, moving them from place to place like I might do with letters in a Scrabble game.

Mei calls out "Fa" and turns up a tile, placing it face up in front of her, then draws another tile, adding it to her hand.

Bernadette says, "Mo fa." They wait for me with patient smiles. I turn to Tony for an explanation.

Tony says, "Fa mean flower. If you have flower, you may draw again."

I point to one of my tiles, a bird perched on a bamboo branch. "Is this one Fa"?

Tony giggles. "No, not Fa. One bamboo."

Bernadette clicks her tongue, "Tony, not fair. I speak English."

"Mo fa." I say. This surprises everyone.

"You pronounce good. Where you learn Chinese"?

I shrug. "Fa and Mo Fa are the only two words I know, so far." This makes Tony and Bernadette laugh. Annie asks a question in Chinese, and Bernadette answers her back. Annie and Mei both laugh, too.

"You funny, Ethan," Tony tells me.

I wasn't trying to be funny, but okay. I'm glad they think I'm funny. It feels good to laugh. Annie says "Leng Fa" and turns up two flowers, drawing two new tiles from the wall.

Next, Mei tosses out a tile face up. Bernadette frowns, looks at her tiles, then reaches for a new tile from the wall. She adds it to her hand and discards a tile face up.

"Deng ha," Tony says, raising a finger. "Ethan, your tile not in order. Here." He reaches around me and moves my tiles into a new configuration. You sort into paai…uh, Bernadette? How you say paai"?

"Suits, like a suit of cards."

"Yes. Suit. This suit bamboo and this suit circles. This

suit called winds. There numbers suit, too, but you don't have any."

"What's this"? I ask, pointing at at tile with the symbol for China in red. "China"?

"How you know China"? Tony is flabbergasted.

"I failed a Japanese class at Columbia University." He laughs and rattles off what I said to Annie and Mei. They quiver with stifled laughter. It's not directed at me, I can tell. They think my answer is funny.

Tony explains, "It funny you learn symbol for China from Japanese. We don't get along. And even more funny because you fail." Then he continues teaching me. "It not just mean China, it also arrow for shooting. We call arrow Red Dragon. Green Dragon and Red Dragon you see both now."

"The first tile Annie drew was Green Dragon, right"?

"Oh. You good. Okay, you need her tile come from Bernadette in discard pile. Take tile, and say "Soeng."

I grab the tile Bernadette threw out. It depicts two stacked bamboo rods, "Soeng. Is this two bamboo"?

Tony nods and points to where it goes, between the bird perched on the bamboo and a tile with three staggered bamboo rods in parallel. "Some rules we have to show why we take tile from middle, but halfway house rules you don't show."

I get it. This is three in a row. 1, 2, 3. I review my hand, the way Tony has arranged it, and I see I should discard the ones on the right. I point to a wind tile with the letter E, and Tony nods. I discard it face down. Tony clucks and turns it right side up, saying "East Wind, Dung Paai." Annie says, "Kong." She draws the East wind and places it face up in front of her hand, and tips forward three more tiles for East Wind. She then draws a tile from the wall, discarding from her hand a tile with both the Arabic numeral and the Chinese symbol for three.

Mei says 'soeng' at the exact moment Bernadette says

'pong.' Mei frowns and Bernadette takes the tile, flipping forward two more number 3 tiles from her hand. It's my turn again.

I wonder why Bernadette won? Tony is a good teacher.

"Bernadette say pong, and pong beats soeng. But you have to say fast. If Bernadette say pong but Annie first say soeng and take tile, it too late."

"So kong is four of a kind, and pong is three of a kind"?

"You scary smart Ethan."

I'm getting the hang of mah jong. The game is a mixture of go fish, bingo and gin rummy. You can have three of a kind, four of a kind, or three in a row. And if you see a tile you need, you shout it out. I'm unclear how the dragons work, or why they are different, but it has to do with how everything is scored. This is fun. I know what to do now. Except I have 13 tiles, and if I get four of a kind I have to say something and draw an extra tile, so I will never have gin rummy. I ask Tony about this conundrum.

"Ethan, how you learn mah jong so fast? It take me ten years to learn. You have three, three, three, three, two with your last tile. We call the pair 'naang zing' - 'pair of eyes'."

We continue playing, but as more pongs and gongs happen, I realize my strategy won't work. I was going for all straights, with a pair of red dragons for the eyes. But Annie ponged the Red Dragon and I have to discard it and try for another.

Annie draws a tile, smiles, and says "sik wu." She turns up all her tiles, and she has won.

Fast as lightning, there are six hands in the middle turning over all of the unused discarded tiles. The remaining walls are broken down and within 30 seconds, the whole set of tiles is face down. I try to give my seat to Tony, but he shakes his head and urges me to continue.

The room fills with loud clattering as we swirl the tiles in a giant whirlpool. Every once in awhile, a tile overturns. Instantly, a hand reaches out, plucks it from the shuffle, then drops it back into the swirling mass face down.

There comes one of those Ouija board moments, silently but mutually agreed upon by all four players, when the swirling stops, and the walls are built. I watch in amazement as Annie, Mei and Bernadette all form a row of 18 tiles in seconds, then a second row with equal speed. My mouth drops when they magically lift all 18 tiles at once and drop one row on top of the other. Then, with more magic, they push the entire wall forward to form one side of the crooked square. I went about things a different way, so I'm straggling. I have been stacking one tile on another, and I have five stacks of two tiles. The whole affair is pretty crooked, and I still have thirteen to go. Annie makes the universal gesture for "May I"? She finishes my wall and straightens it, then pushes it forward to form the last side.

On the second shuffle, I try to stack eighteen tiles at once, pushing them together with intense force. They lift into the air. I am amazed. But I hesitate to marvel at my magic, and the whole row flies apart in an explosion of tiles, which is followed by an explosion of laughter all around the table. Annie remakes my top row of eighteen, taking face down tiles from another wall, while Bernadette and Mei remove the upturned tiles and shuffle them into other parts of the wall.

On the third shuffle, I use both pinkies to apply pressure evenly along the edges of the tile. I stack in one movement, then push forward in another. And I am hooked now.

On the fourth game, my strategy pays off. I declare "sik wu" and turn up all my tiles. We play long into the night, until the counselor on duty tells us to stop because the shuffling will wake the other clients.

Tony tells me how in his home growing up, they used to play mah jong in the basement on a thick blanket. They used the blanket to muffle the sound of the illegal game. "Illegal? How can playing a game be illegal"?

"In Hong Kong, we play for money. Big money. People lose everything. My father lose everything. So we go to America to San Francisco. New life, new world."

"How do you win or lose money in mah jong"?

"I teach you another time. This game fun only."

"Is your father safe now"?

Tony closes his eyes and shakes his head. "They find him many years ago. When I little boy."

We wait for the memory to pass. I would apologize, but it won't help in this situation. He takes three deep breaths and smiles at me.

"So I teach you how points work next time, okay"?

"You bet."

CHAPTER 14 - INTERRUPTED

I give my usual knock at the door, and Chance says, "Ethan, 'that you"?

Chance is sprawled out reading Teenage Mutant Ninja Turtles. He lifts his olive eyes from the page to look at me. He wears a big grin; it could be interpreted in a half-dozen ways: He's happy to see me; He was enjoying the comic book; He's annoyed and hiding it behind a smile; He's into me; He's trying to seduce me; He's remembering a great day at the beach...I should just ask, but I'm scared.

"You find a vacation in there, Ethan"? He points to my purloined copy of Let's Go! Mexico 1986. I hand it to him. "You speak Spanish, right"?

"Yeah, actually, not very well but I do."

"We should go." He looks at me again with the same smile.

"Why are you smiling"? Even as the words leave my mouth, I realize I should have said it when I walked in the room, not now, and not in an accusatory tone. Chance's smile turns into a frown. I turn away embarrassed. Can I fix this, or is he mad now?

"Ethan, I'm smiling because I am high on life." When I

raise the courage to look at him again, the smile is back. "Let's look at this book together little buddy." I am Gilligan sharing a hammock with the Skipper.

He sits beside me on my bed, and I can smell his leather jacket. He's leaning pretty close, but it's not what I want it to be. He's just making sure I can read the same thing he's reading. There is this pleasant musky odor under the leather, and I know it's Chance's sweat. Why does it smell good? Mine smells like the fish market in Chinatown.

The book is so massive, I don't know where to start. There's the big introductory section about how to get there and how to get around. They say traveler's checks are the safest and least troublesome means of carrying your funds. Cash is just a huge headache. I don't know how or where you buy traveler's checks. Plus don't they cost like 3.75 per 100 dollars? How stupid. I'll take my chances with cash.

We look at the section on Chiapas. I want to see Palenque.

"Have you ever seen the stuff they have in Palenque"? Chance is reading my mind. "They have this carving of a king on a spaceship."

I perk up, "Yes, as a matter of fact. We studied the tomb of Pakal in my Art History class and I have wanted to see it ever since."

"Dude, you should totally go to Palenque." Chance dog-ears the Palenque page. It's a library book, but what the hell. I think I'm stealing it anyway. I noticed he didn't say "we should go." I keep my mouth shut and hide my disappointment

"What about Mexico City"? Chance asks. "It's one of the largest cities in the world. Let's make sure you go there." The section on Mexico City is over 20 pages, so Chance puts a dried eucalyptus leaf as a bookmark.

"And you should see the cultural heart of Mexico, so you have to go to Guadalajara. The place is Mexico on a stick."

"Yeah," I agree. "Isn't it where the Mariachis come from"?

Although it is a stupid question, Chance is gracious, "Yeah they have a whole giant square in the middle of town where the Mariachis gather to find work at weddings and whatnot."

I remember my situation, how stuck I am, and hang my head. Chance shakes me by the shoulder, "Ethan, what's up"?

Fighting back tears, I say, "This is fun, but there's just no way I could ever go. I'm fucking crazy and I'm locked up in a halfway house. I have nowhere to go."

Chance smiles the same delicious smile and says in a deep voice, "Ethan, you can do anything you want. You have nothing to lose."

"Except my sanity."

"Sorry, you already lost it, along with just about everything else." I glare at Chance, but his mirthful face wipes away the anger and replaces it with laughter.

"Seriously, Ethan. You don't have a wife or kids, no mortgage, no job – you will never have a better time in your life to go on a wild adventure."

"I'll think about it."

"Who knows, maybe I'll go with you. It sounds like a fucking blast."

I lie in my bed enjoying the image of me falling asleep on Chance's shoulder on a train in Mexico. As I drift towards slumber, I feel him watching me. I wonder what he sees when he looks at me? I only know it is not what I see in him. He finds me repulsive.

I turn towards him and lock eyes. He is so handsome, it hurts. Without prompting, he says, "Ethan, you are a good looking kid. You don't mind me saying so, right"?

Before I can catch my breath to gasp, the door comes open and Janis walks in with some white dude I've never seen before. He is short and stout. He wears dress slacks and a white t-shirt.

"This is Calvin. He'll be taking this bed." Janis points to an empty bed I hadn't noticed until now, then turns tail and leaves us to get acquainted. Chance rolls his eyes and sighs. As I stand, Calvin breezes past Chance, ignoring him, and pumps my hand. "Calvin, and you are…"

"Ethan."

"Yeah, Ethan. Janis told me. So you and me are gonna be bunkies." Calvin has an accent somewhere between Chicago and Texas. He could be from Nebraska.

"We are"? I'm not good at hiding my disappointment.

"Yeah, just you and me."

"And Chance," I gesture towards Chance, who snores to avoid the conversation.

He glances in Chance's direction, then shrugs. "This is a beautiful room." Calvin has a rustic charm.

"So, where were you before this, Calvin"?

"Probably the same place you were. San Francisco General."

"You came straight from the hospital"? I look over at Chance, who no longer pretends to sleep. He's asleep. Chance is not a people person, and Calvin is.

"Yes. I was easy to fix, you know, just needed my lithium levels sorted out and now I'm right as rain." He has a definite twang to his speech.

"Calvin, where are you from?"

"Oklahoma."

"The Sooner State," I say, making idle conversation.

"Why yes it is. How did you know?"

"Calvin, you will soon learn there is an extraordinary stack of trivia piled in my brain. Your state bird is the scissor-tailed flycatcher, right?"

"Ethan, I think you might be a genius, unless you ever lived in Oklahoma, why would you know something so obscure?"

"In fifth grade we had to learn all 50 State Capitals,

Nicknames, Mottos, Birds, Tallest Mountains, State Animals...you get the picture."

"And you still remember them?"

"Is the Bison the state animal of Oklahoma, and does it shit on the plains?"

Calvin loses his smile. "I don't like vulgar language. It's not appropriate."

Great. I am living with Calvin the Calvinist and Chance the misanthrope. What if Calvin is a big homophobe?

"Calvin, what brought you to San Francisco"? The question is a good opener to figure out which way their wind blows on the whole gay thing.

"One day I just stopped my medicine and an inner voice told me to head West. So here I am."

Hmmm. Not enough info. "How do you like it here? Have you seen much of the city?"

"Oh San Francisco is pretty and all. A lot of weird people, though."

"I'm weird, Calvin. You are too, if you're in the mental health system, right?"

Calvin gives a snort. "Maybe, but I'm not weird in that way!"

"Yeah, but I am. Is it a problem"?

"Hell no! I don't care what you do as long as you don't do it to me." It's an acceptable answer, so I fall silent to let him open up more.

"I mean, half my friends back home in OKC are queer. You guys are so much more interesting than the cowboys and oilmen, you know"?

"We prefer to use the term 'gay' in San Francisco."

Calvin is horrified at his faux pas. "Gosh, Ethan, I'm so sorry. I forget it's a bad word because it's just how you say it back in Oklahoma, even my quee-- my gay friends use that word." I am charmed by his contrition. He's no great prize, but living with him won't be so bad. I doubt Chance agrees.

"No apology necessary. I was pointing out the local custom."

"Whew! Well, it's late. Gotta get ready." Calvin waddles over to his bed and unpacks his clothes into a small dresser. He removes his shirt, folds it, and puts it on the ground He takes off his shoes and aligns them at the edge of his bed. This takes several adjustments. Next are dress slacks, so now he's just wearing a wife beater, BVDs and black socks.

I look over at Chance to see if he's watching, but he can sleep through anything. When I look back, Calvin is naked except for his black socks. Toothbrush in hand, he walks into the hallway and shuts himself in the hall bathroom. I hear strains of country songs garbled by a toothbrush. I wish Chance were awake to witness this.

Calvin comes swinging back into the room, oblivious to his nudity. I marvel at the level of comfort with his body he must possess to wander the halls naked. He's going to get into trouble.

"I'm a grower, not a shower," Calvin says. As if to prove his point, he plays with himself to fluff up a bit. Indeed, it grows bigger. Then overcome with some mysterious shame, he covers himself and jumps under the covers. He turns to me and says, "Quit looking."

He removes one black sock and throws it out onto the floor. I hear a rhythmic thwacking sound. The other sock will serve as a receptacle to contain his eventual release. Calvin's moral compass is lopsided. After a few minutes, Calvin moans, then turns out the light.

"Ethan, can you turn out the other light please"?

I don't want Calvin leaving man-dribble all over the room, so I do as he asks. I hope this isn't a regular routine.

Calvin snores. I need to buy ear plugs. Lying in the dark, unable to sleep, I remember the magic moment destroyed when Calvin came in the room. I'm filled with hope now, because Chance has let on he finds me attractive. Not just attractive...I'm good looking. He’s a sexy motherfucker.

CHAPTER 15 - WORK

My first night at Sweet Inspirations takes me for a twirl. I meet my co-workers: Heather and Liz. Heather is a new-waver; she has an asymmetrical bob and wears a checkered blouse with a pink miniskirt. She's a music lover. Her favorites are TinTin, BowWowWow and Adam and the Ants. "They're assonant and alliterative," I tell her.

Heather wrinkles her nose. "What do you mean"?

"Assonance is when a vowel sound repeats, like ow, ow, ow or in in. Alliteration is when the consonant repeats, so like wow wow and T T and Adam and Ant."

"Whatever, dude, I just like the music."

Liz has dyed black hair and piercing blue eyes, with a Texas accent. She is warmer than Heather, and more interested in what I do and who I am. "Damon tells us you are experienced. You've served before"?

"Yeah, I worked at a bar in New York called the Milk Bar."

Heather leans in, curious, and asks, "Did they serve milk"?

"No. It was named after a bar in A Clockwork Orange."

"You mean the Korova Milk Bar"? Liz is well-read.

Heather squints at Liz.

Liz explains, "It's this great science fiction book and even better movie. The thugs all go to a bar where they drink milk laced with drugs and do crazy shit."

"The New York Milk Bar was pretty tame compared to the one in the novel," I offer. I like my co-workers right away, even Heather.

Damon shows me how to make a layered latte. First, you put cold extra rich Vitamin D milk into a stainless steel pitcher - not too much, because once it heats up, you can't use it again - it won't work. Rotate the valve and keep the steam nozzle right at the surface of the milk, so it "blows bubbles." Like when you were a kid and you blew bubbles with a straw. Only these bubbles are tiny, and they act like meringue. What you get is a pitcher filled half with hot milk, half with foam. Next, you pack this heavy scoop called the 'portafilter' with ground espresso, and press it on the built-in tamper. The scoop seals like a pressure cooker over a steam valve called the gasket. The steam runs through the coffee, and drips out of the two spouts at the bottom of the portafilter. You put a teacup under the spouts to catch the drippings.

Meanwhile, you pour hot milk into a tall glass mug, about to the halfway mark. Next, using a long spoon, you scoop a bunch of foam on top of the hot milk. Damon is a very good teacher. The teacupful of espresso comes next.

"Don't just dump the espresso in, you need to make it cling to the inside edge of the mug, like this." Damon tips the teacup gently and lets the espresso drip down the outside of the cup until it makes contact with the inside edge of the glass mug. A miracle happens. The espresso passes through the foam unfettered and floats on top of the milk, underneath the foam.

"If you're making a macchiato, you're done. But if this is a caffe latte, you have to scoop one more bit of foam to hide this stain where the coffee passed through the foam."

Damon puts another dollop of foam, and voila! The three layer treat is complete.

It's a happy surprise this is easy for me. Damon watches me make one latte, and declares me ready to serve. He isn't quick to hand out compliments, but I can tell he's impressed. Liz and Heather still can't do it, so they take orders and bus tables. I'm at the register. I make fun coffee drinks, cut slices of cake, and smile at the hot guys, a harmless flirtation which often leads to better tips. This is San Francisco, after all.

I catch Liz during a moment of relative quiet, "I hope you aren't mad at me for working the espresso machine. I know you and Heather are both in line ahead of me for the position."

"Did Damon tell you that"? She smiles. "We graduated. I prefer working both sides of the counter and picking up shit. Making espressos is easy - I just don't want Damon to make me do it."

"Heather the same thing, then? She's faking it"?

"Nah, she genuinely sucks at running the espresso machine. She always burns herself on the steam."

Throughout the night, we have to keep the steam nozzles clean and free from stuck on milk residue. This involves rubbing up and down the nozzle with a damp rag in long strokes, just like the cute guy at Cafe Soma. I do my best not to make this cleaning look too sexual, but it's a challenge. Whether I go fast, slow, light speed - there is no denying it looks like I'm giving the espresso maker a hand job.

Even on a weeknight, Sweet Inspirations is very busy. Cake and coffee fly over the counter and tips overflow. Damon grabs singles and sells them back to the register while I keep the customers' orders moving.

The teamwork is something different from my earlier jobs. Instead of being isolated and put on a task all by myself, I have coworkers who act like partners. Heather and

Liz take turns switching from busing tables to taking orders and running the register. It's an unusual feeling of camaraderie. I mention this to Damon. "Yeah, I could tell from the moment you came in asking about the job you were gonna fit right in. It's why I hired you." He has no idea; even though I live in a mansion on Jackson street, I'm no rich kid. I live in a mental facility and don't want anyone to know.

At the end of the night, there is $118.00 in the tip jar. We split it four ways - Damon is meticulous with the money, breaking fives into ones and ones into quarters. We each get $29.25. It's more money than I've had since I went to the hospital.

It's late. I walk Fillmore to Jackson, enjoying the posh surroundings. I pass a very busy bar called "The Alta Plaza." There's a piano inside, and a chorus of male voices sings showtunes. I want to go in and spend all my money on a drink. Then I look at my espresso-stained Vans and my grubby jeans, and think better of it. Note to self: do laundry tomorrow morning.

Back at Conard House, I have to rap on the door so the night counselor can let me in. It's a dude named Brad whom I only met once before.

"Ethan, it's way past curfew." He isn't mad.

"I got a night job just down the street at Sweet Inspirations."

"Very nice. I wish I could afford to go there! I get my coffee at the donut shop. Well, don't let me keep you. Don't forget your meds."

"Thanks, Brad."

I decide to go via the back stairs, which requires me to pass through the common room. I'm looking for somewhere to stash my cash. On the games shelf, there's a box of Jenga tiles; most of them are missing. This is pretty good. But I don't like the collapsing tower imagery accompanying such a box, so I keep looking. Behind a stack of magazines there is a dark orange tea tin "Grandmother's Tea." On the outside, a silhouette shows a Japanese chashitsu set against a stylized image of Mount Fuji. The paint is worn in a pattern resembling steam. It suggests there's a Grandma inside the tea room boiling water in a cauldron. Inside are just the dregs of a few old tea leaves. I don't know where this came from, but it will work. I am superstitious about removing the tea leaves, so I lay the money folded on top of the leaves. This is my Mexico money. I shepherd it to the room hidden in my coat. Calvin is snoring. Chance is downstairs watching the Tonight Show. After a few furtive glances to ensure there are no hidden assassins watching from the shadows, I stash Grandmother's Tea in the far recesses of my duffel bag. It is about as safe as you're gonna get it in a halfway house.

Outside my second story window, I can see a few city lights. I think about the hundreds of rich Pacific Heights people tucked away in their mansions and apartments. I wonder how they figured it out. They are making tens of thousands of dollars a month. I am excited because I just brought home thirty dollars. A darkness overcomes me and I lose hope. I fucked up my life; I will never be able to live in one of these mansions except as a client at a halfway house. The irony stings and draws tears.

There's a hand on my shoulder. I didn't hear him come in. Chance sits on my bed and holds me while I throw a pity party for myself.

"Hey, hey little buddy. What's wrong?"

"I fucked up. I fucked it all up. I'm never gonna be anyone or anything."

"That's not true."

"How do I escape this trap? I'm in a very posh, permissive mental hospital. But I have nowhere else to go."

"This is just a temporary prison, Ethan." I notice how safe I feel as he holds me. I take advantage of his kindness and put my head on his shoulder. He doesn't pull away in disgust. He just runs his fingers through my hair.

"I don't see a way out. It's an endless loop."

Chance pats my head and squeezes me in his arms. "It's not. I promise you. You are not very sick. You're getting out of here."

I pull away from Chance to give him his breathing space. He brushes a thumb across my cheek to wipe away a stray tear.

I gesture to the many mansions out my window. "How do they do it, Chance? How do they make all their money"?

"They buy low, sell high."

"What do you mean?"

"I don't know. Just something my Dad used to say. If I understood it, I wouldn't be here." He chuckles and gives me a noogie. "Alright, buddy, time to rest. Tomorrow will be better than tonight."

As I drift into hazy slumber, I wonder if there's any way Chance could be my boyfriend. He likes to tease me. He doesn't want me the way I want him. Same fucking story, different dorm.

CHAPTER 16 - CASHING CHECKS

My bankroll grows each night as I work at Sweet Inspirations. Grandmother's Tea is filling to overflowing, and my paychecks are piling up. I need to bring them to a check cashing place so GA doesn't find out about them. If I deposit them in my savings account, GA will know. There is a sleazy C&C check-cashing place on Fillmore and O'Farrell. People go to C&C to collect their food stamps. There's always a line of foreign women waiting out front asking if you want to sell. They give $60.00 for $110.00 worth of food stamps -- enough to buy dope, rock, crystal or whatever the recipient has deemed more important than food.

Chance volunteers to walk me there so I don't get mugged. I have several weeks' worth of paychecks now. Each is worth about $85.00 after taxes. Ronald Reagan made service employees pay tax on tips. Even though I am not a waiter, I have to pay a tax on the tips I would have received if I were. Most nights I get about $20.00 in tips from the jar. They tax me on over $100.00 based on what comes into the till for the owners. And I can't get it back. This explains why my paycheck is so small. At least they add up over time.

On our walk down Fillmore, Chance and I pass the glitzy shops. There's Betsey Johnson, where I would buy my clothes if I had money. It's all women's clothes, but I can pull off a couple of Betsey Johnson jackets or leggings. There's Z Gallerie, a two story department store carrying fancy furniture, art reproductions like "Night Owls" by Edward Hopper or a 1/16 scale copy of Rodin's "The Thinker." There's flatware and china in ultra moderne Memphis shapes and colors. They have far too many couch cushions and a selection of rugs worth six months labor at Sweet Inspirations..

Chance shakes his head. "Do you really want any of this stuff"?

"Nah. I mean, it would be nice, but I don't need it."

"But you want it." He gives a serious stare.

"Sure I want it. I want world peace. I want an artist's studio by the sea."

As we make our way, our animated conversation must appear to be an argument, because the pedestrians give us a wide berth as they pass us. I suppose they don't often see two lunatics engaged in heavy discourse.

As we cross Bush, the neighborhood grows less and less toney. There's a black-owned seafood restaurant, a holdout from the days when the Fillmore was ruled by jazz and soul. Fried Catfish wafts into the street, making my stomach growl. We run into our first panhandler. The cops don't mess with panhandlers below Bush. Plus there's the Kabuki Cinema on our right, drawing a lot of foot traffic to one place - a panhandler's motherlode.

Inside the check-cashing center, a motley line of financially unwell people snakes around a series of stanchions leading to a row of bullet proof glass windows.

The clock ticks slower in desolate places. C&C Check Cashing smells of garbage and urine-soaked undergarments. The stench causes the clock to leave snail trails. There are at least 15 people ahead of us. Chance tells me part of his story to keep me amused.

"You see, I thought I was the Mayor, so I went to the rotunda at City Hall to make an announcement, but the police got the wrong idea. They thought I was a jumper. I was just there to announce some governmental reforms to make life in San Francisco much better."

"Like what?"

"Well, gay marriage, for one."

"Gay marriage? How sick were you? It will never happen. There are way too many bible thumpers, even here. I mean look what happened to Harvey Milk."

"Yeah, I was actually gonna propose a national holiday for him, too. But I didn't have the opportunity."

"Besides, why are you so interested in gay marriage? Does it affect you in any way?" I didn't mean to make it sound like a challenge, but it does.

Chance goes on the defensive. "I mean, I don't want to live in a world where one group of people, mostly idiots, decides a much smaller group of people are less than human."

I'm touched by this. "Is marriage what makes us human?"

"Dignity makes us human."

"Would you shut up!" An angry little man in Charles Nelson Reilly glasses and a mud-stained London Fog raincoat turns and glares at us. "We deserve a little peace."

I shrug and glance at Chance, who shrugs back. We await our turn in silence.

After C&C is done extracting their usurious fee, I am left with a little over $500.00 in cash. I'm glad Chance is here to protect me. There are several ne'er do wells lurking nearby who would love nothing more than to jump me for my money. Chance pats his leather jacket pocket and flashes a switchblade. We're safe.

On the way back, we stop inside the Goodwill on Geary

and Fillmore. This is where all the rich people's stuff rolls down the hill to be sold to poor people. I haven't gone thrifting since before the hospital. This is my all time favorite hobby.

Chance and I wind back and forth through the racks and shelves examining each item for its potential value and actual price. If I had my own place, I would buy antiques here. As it is, I'm just cruising the knick-knacks, hoping for a small but valuable find. Chance presents me with a snowglobe of San Francisco. Of course, it doesn't snow in San Francisco, so this one has sequins and glitter instead. Come close to a drag queen on Gay Pride, and you will be drenched in a rain of sequins, glitter, and loose rhinestones.

"You want me to buy you this, Ethan?"

If the globe were clear, well made, not full of some kind of algae, I might want it. How do I tell him 'no' politely?

"If you find one for Palenque, then I'll take it." It wasn't too rude, right? Chance puts it back and keeps looking.

Then he surprises me. He finds an old 1960's Capodimonte porcelain model of a Vespa with a guy sitting on it who looks like Chance, down to the leather jacket! "Ethan, you gotta let me get this for you."

I want it, but it's a portrait of him. "Don't you want it? It looks like you."

Chance shakes his head, "I look at myself every day in the mirror. This is for you to remember me when I'm not around." It's syrupy and romantic. But it's a nice gesture.

I perk up, "Well hells yeah, get me the Vespa. I'll put it on my dresser."

We trudge up Fillmore on the southeast side of the street. These stores are more geared towards new mothers. Corduroy jumpers and shabby chic bassinets compete for window space in the cluttered mommy shops. We reach La Mediterranee, the Greek/Lebanese restaurant. Chance insists on buying me lunch. I've never been before.

"This one is the annex. The real one is in the Castro. But this food will make you cry. It's so fucking good." I remember Damon saying something about it at work.

We order Mezze - mixed appetizers to share. It doesn't look like much food, but together we can't finish it all. Chance pays the check. This is what it must be like to go on a date with someone. I've never dated, just tricked with one night stands. It feels safe and warm.

Upstairs, I place Chance's gift on the dresser where I can see it from my bed. I dig out my tin of Grandmother's Tea and add the fresh wad of bills to the stash. I wish there were someplace safer, but this is it.

CHAPTER 17 - POMODORO CRUDO

Conard House has a basement, a first floor, a second floor and an attic converted into bedrooms. Our room is in the attic. There are sections of the room where the roof angles all the way down to the floor. You can sleep in a bed, but there's still wasted space. Chance seems to prefer a mattress that wedges right into the spot where the roof meets the floor. I want to crawl over there and cuddle with him. But I can't. I watch his chest rise and fall. I need to be close to him. He won't let me. I disgust him. He would never want a fat ugly lunatic like me.

I can tell him how I feel while he sleeps. That's safe.

"Chance," softly, "I know I'm an ugly piece of shit and you're a god, but would you ever consider being more than a friend"? Chance's soft breath causes his chest to rise and fall in a soothing rhythm that makes me feel sleepy. I continue. "I want to have a pride parade with you everywhere we go. I would hold your oil-stained hand and you would take my little hand and we would be together. In love. Just you and me, on my Vespa, riding down the Great Highway."

Calvin is snoring. The problem with being so crazy is

that I forget stuff constantly, like going to Walgreens for earplugs. I search through my few possessions to see if I can fashion earplugs out of raw materials. Toilet paper, that's what we use.

I tiptoe out into the hall. We're allowed to go to the bathroom; I don't know why I feel like I need to be sneaky. I roll toilet tissue onto my hand and return to make my remedy. After several attempts, I get the right width and length of tissue. I can still hear Calvin, but the noise blends with traffic and other sounds that are now muffled. I can sleep.

Except I can't. I look at Chance, and he's looking back.

"Hey." He grins.

"Oh, hey." I'm busted.

"Can I get some of that toilet paper"?

"How long have you been awake"? I unroll a few sheets. Chance twists them into perfectly shaped earplugs. He is a mechanic.

"I haven't been able to sleep." Oh, shit. Was he not asleep?

"So, were you wide awake, then"?

"Ethan, I heard what you said. It's beautiful, really. I wish you had the guts to say that to me when you know I'm awake.

"Okay then, I will. I love you."

The room tastes like sour milk.

Chance puts the earplugs in and rolls facing the junction of wall and ceiling. I watch his back for a minute before I curse myself into oblivion.

Chance waves me over.

"What"? I'm fighting back tears.

"Let's cuddle."

In bed, he gently takes my arm and puts it around his chest, holding it there tightly. I would normally pop a boner at this point, but the vibe he gives off is completely different. It's deep, romantic friendship. It's not what I want, but I'll take table scraps.

Chance smells like Jovan Musk. The gentle rise and fall of his chest lulls me to sleep.

In the morning, Calvin is standing over me. Chance is gone.

"What are you doing there"?

"Nothing." I crawl off the mattress and get to my feet with as much dignity as the situation allows.

"Care to join me for breakfast"? Calvin's offer is kind. I want to decline, but I don't want to hurt his feelings.

At the breakfast table he shakes his head and laughs.

"What"?

"You, Ethan. The look on your face when you woke up."

I blush.

"There it is again"! Calvin cackles.

Despite his many quirks, his annoying twang and his abrasive manner, Calvin is not a bad person. He's one of the good ones. I'm not saying I'm fond of him, but I don't mind being his friend. I learn more about him as we eat soggy Cheerios with whole milk and too much sugar.

"My first hospitalization was in college," he tells me. "I thought I had uncovered an alien/Christian conspiracy."

"Details."

"Oh, well I was at ORU."

"Is that Oklahoma Regional University?"

"No, Silly. Oral Roberts University in Tulsa. Anyway, they got this prayer tower with an antenna that supposedly communicates with God."

"And they locked you up"?

"I know, right? Yeah so I was having my first manic episode and they put a huge balloon on top of the antenna for some reason. Or at least that's what I saw."

"Who's they?"

"I guess the Regents of the University, and Oral himself."

"I've always thought Oral was a weird name to give a boy, or a girl."

Calvin nods. "Yeah, and so lightning struck the balloon and I saw alien ships. Please don't think I'm crazy."

"I don't think you're crazy. I know we're both crazy and you're in good company. Keep going."

"So the aliens saw me see them and they came after me. They were everywhere."

"How did you recognize them"?

"The same way we all do. One eye up, one eye straight ahead."

I drop my spoon. Calvin hands me a paper towel. I start to quiver with fear. That's the people on the number 27 bus.

"Calvin, I know which bus they take."

"The 27, right"?

There is an expression, 'to feel one's heart beating in one's chest.' This is what they mean. Fear washes over me.

"Shhh! They get mad when you talk about them!"

Calvin shrugs. "We're protected here."

"How"?

"They're allergic to wood. This whole place would give them hives."

Thinking back on my encounters with the wall-eyed aliens, I realize it was always in concrete or metal structures, like the jail or a bus.

"Okay, but they're not real, Calvin. We are crazy, and we made them up."

"They're as real as your cereal bowl. They're as real as that toaster."

"No, that's why they give us lithium."

"Most people can't see them. I mean, they see them, but they don't know like you and me."

"So I took us down a rabbit hole. You were at Oral Roberts University, and…"?

"I took my clothes off and climbed the praying hands

sculpture. They had to call the fire department to get me down."

"And you went to jail"?

"No, they took me straight to the hospital in an ambulance. The police didn't want to get involved." Calvin put his soup bowl in the sink.

"Lucky. I got 5150'ed."

"Jail is a shitty place to be when you're on a manic high."

I figured it was worth asking Calvin about some other weirdness. "So, when I was in jail, I could use my psychic energy to open electronic locks. Did you have anything like that"?

"Not really. I believe it though. It's crazy energy, the best kind."

Calvin teaches mathematics when he's not perched naked atop a giant bronze statue of praying hands.

"Did you leave your students behind to come here"?

"Yeah, but they already had a substitute because I was on medical leave."

"What kind of math do you teach"?

"Oh, I'm mostly pre-Algebra, Algebra, Trigonometry and pre-Calculus. Geometry is for pussies."

"Where were you teaching"?

"OKC Community College. Not the smartest bunch of Sooners, but they learned."

"Are you going to teach here in the City"?

Calvin frowns. Maybe I'm asking too many questions. But then, "Well, I hadn't really thought of it. Do you think they need a bipolar Math teacher"?

"Most schools will take whatever they can get. Especially Math. My friend Wanda used to teach English. She might know."

Calvin brightens. "Would you ask her"?

I shrug. "Right now. I'll call her at BUSTCo."

The Berwick US Trading Company (BUSTCo) is an

importer of brass plumbing fixtures. Wanda is an Aquarian so she took the job to be a water bearer. Plus, she says, her part of fortune is in Aries, and brass is ruled by Aries. She has done extremely well for herself there. She has an 800 number so it's easy to reach her.

"BUSTCo, this is Wanda speaking."

"Wanda, hey, it's Ethan." There is a loud shriek and peals of laughter. It is a good feeling to be loved so intensely by a good friend. The noises make Calvin smile.

"Ethan, it's so good to hear your voice. What's going on"?

"Oh, nothing, I have a friend who teaches math and I thought you might know someone who can help him."

"Is it that boy you like? I thought he repairs motorcycles."

"Nah, that's Chance. This is Calvin. He teaches math, and he's pretty good."

"Okay, hmmm. What sign is he"?

"What's your sign"?

Calvin grins. "Stop sign."

Wanda doesn't lose a beat. "Okay, that means he's a Sagittarius because they never believe in anything."

"So, Sagittarius"?

Calvin nods dumbly.

"Perfect. He and Kari will get along like a house on fire. She's a Leo. Tell him to call Kari and tell her I sent him."

I give Kari's number to Calvin, with Wanda's instructions.

"Is Kari hiring"?

"No, no, no. She's a psychic. She doesn't charge. She'll read him and tell him exactly where he needs to go. He'll never go if you tell him that, so just say she's well-connected, if he asks."

"Can I go see her"?

"She's an astro-bigot. She hates Pisces. We may lose our friendship over it. Besides, aren't you cooking up some scheme to go to Mexico"?

"How did you hear about that"?

"You just sent me a psychic fax."

Wanda is an incredible, powerful psychic. Not like my mom, who uses her psychic energy to exert power over people and make red lights turn green. Wanda is in touch with the full spectrum of light.

I leave Calvin on his call with Kari and enter the Kitchen. Kathleen smiles. She is dicing tomatoes, adding them to an enormous glass bowl.

"Whatcha making?"

"Pasta alla Pomodoro Crudo. Can you squeeze some garlic for me?"

"I thought we weren't cooking until tomorrow night."

"You have to let the tomatoes, capers, olives, basil and garlic sit overnight. Tomorrow night we just make garlic bread and cook the penne."

"When do we cook the sauce?"

"'Crudo' means 'raw'. It comes from Sicily where it gets horribly hot in summer. You don't want to have a lot of stuff cooking all day long. So you cook pasta and add it to the tomatoes when it's hot. The pasta cooks the sauce."

I squeeze two bulbs of garlic into the bowl of finely diced tomatoes. As I finish chopping green olives, Kathleen dumps a full jar of capers in, and adds two cups of olive oil. We both tear basil into little bits. The olives go in last. She stirs the whole concoction with an industrial wooden spoon, covers the bowl with six long strips of plastic wrap, and puts it in the giant fridge. The large scale of the kitchen equipment creates the comical illusion that Kathleen is an elf.

"Tomorrow, before we do any cooking, we take that bowl out so it can warm up."

I nod.

"They only had fake Parmesan cheese at Safeway, so we'll have to make do." Kathleen indicates a collection of green foil cardboard tubes that say, 'Scotch Buy Parmesan Cheese - Italian Style' in big letters, then 'A pasteurized cheese recipe' in much smaller script.

"My mom says it has wood chips in it."

Kathleen nods. "I don't doubt it. But it tastes a lot like cheese, so it will work."

Making dinner is easy tonight. Kathleen took the huge bowl of tomatoes out of the fridge around 3pm when she got back from Day Treatment, so it's at room temperature now. I can smell the garlic from the other side of the kitchen. Kathleen puts on a giant pot of water to boil. We cut the giant loaves of Columbo sourdough bread in half lengthwise. We spread a mixture of crushed garlic and spreadable margarine liberally on each half. The oven can take six loaves at a time; we have 12 loaves. The bread cooks for 10 minutes until it's charred on the edges. I cut each half into 6 pieces and toss them into a big bowl lined with clean dish towels. Meanwhile, Kathleen throws a huge handful of salt into the industrial-size pot of boiling water. She immediately dumps in box after box of Golden Grain penne. The pot foams up but doesn't boil over.

The box says to cook it for 11 minutes, but Kathleen pours out most of the water at nine minutes. She ladles the condensed liquids from the enormous bowl of tomatoes into the pot and cooks the pasta for another two minutes. Then she drains it, and dumps the whole hot pile into the bowl. Instantly, a garlicky basil vapor rises with the steam. It causes my mouth to water involuntarily. The bowl is nearly filled to the top, so Kathleen stirs it carefully with the giant serving spoon. I catch any bits that fall over the edge and add them back to the bowl. The second batch of garlic bread is ready; I cut it and fill the big bowl of bread to the top, covering it with a towel.

First in line is Rick, a fifty-year old black guy with Schizophrenia. He takes three pieces of garlic bread and three giant spoonfuls of penne. "Hey, where's the meat? I need meat with every meal."

Kathleen smiles sweetly and hands him a cylinder of parmesan cheese. "Take this back to the table with you, please."

Rick grumbles and shuffles off to the dining room. He is the toughest customer. Everyone else moans and groans with joy as they gorge themselves on Kathleen's Sicilian/Californian cooking.

I look around, but Chance is not here. I save him a bowl and two pieces of garlic bread.

I've already managed to sock away a couple hundred dollars from my tips at Sweet Inspirations. No one at Conard House knows how to account for the money, so they can't factor it in when extracting the rent from my GA check, which would only leave 15 dollars for me to buy cigarettes, get my hair cut, buy snacks, or whatever else people do with 15 dollars a month. As the pile of money grows, I am leery of keeping my whole stash in one place. I consider carrying half in my wallet. I don't want to get mugged on the three block walk between Conard House and Sweet Inspirations. Chance offers to keep half in his backpack. I can't think of anywhere safer, so I agree.

My secret Mexico vacation makes the days fly by. I tell Janis I want to go on a trip to Mexico with "a friend" (I don't want to get Chance in trouble) and she says it would be "AMA" or "Against Medical Advice." She's pretty cool, so she adds, "I'm not a doctor, so I can give non-medical advice. That sounds like a pretty fucking cool trip to me. But you need to think about where you will live when you come back. You should wait a few months until after you're in a co-op. You don't want to return homeless."

Great advice. If I leave early, I will need to talk to my Mother about crashing at her apartment. I make a mental note to do so, with an added mental pang of dread.

Tonight it's Mah Jong. Shirley Mae and Tony Ha form

two sides with me and Bernadette. I have gotten pretty good at Mah Jong, and I find playing it takes my mind off of other stuff. Pong! Pick up for three of a kind. Kong! Four of a kind. Bernadette chatters away like a sports announcer, the Howard Cosell of Mah Jong.

I do have a good head for numbers and cards. I inherited it from the Jewish side of the family. They were all card sharks on riverboats in the South, riding the Mississippi making money for the family by counting cards and bluffing. I just know which cards have fallen and which are still in play. I can't help it. Les Jeux Sont Faits.

Chance leans in and makes a signal for me to meet him upstairs. I excuse myself from the table at the end of the round. Bernadette still wants to play, so I let Helen Ka have my seat. I run to the room, where Chance is waiting.

"Ethan, my time here is up. I'm leaving in a few days. I gave it some thought, and I want to go to Mexico in January. I would love it if you came with me."

A thousand thoughts bombard me at once. Chance wants to go with me to Mexico. He used the word 'love' in a sentence about me. Chance is leaving me at Conard House all alone. It's nearly Christmas, so this is coming too soon. If I go with him, I would be leaving the program early.

"Why January"?

"It's the best time for me. I can take time off. Nobody rides Vespas in January in San Francisco."

"Yeah, but I'll lose my spot for a co-op apartment. I have to stay until March."

"A while ago, you asked me how to break out of this jail. How to escape the loop. This trip is the way."

He has an excellent point. I'm being too cautious, keeping myself trapped in the mental health world. "You know what, Chance? Fuck it. Let's go."

CHAPTER 18 - TICKETS AND COFFEE

The Greyhound station on Seventh Street is a filthy shithole, but they have some tickets to great destinations. I buy my ticket to San Diego and a transfer ticket to Mexicali. This will cost 42 dollars, more than the entire train fare to Guadalajara, Mexico DF, and the Yucatan from Mexicali. Amazing. Chance buys his ticket and we're set. We leave January 15 for San Diego, transfer to Calexico, then cross on foot to Mexicali. We can buy our train ticket there. Janis isn't going to be happy about this, but I think it's the right thing to do, given my age and ability with the Spanish language. We can see so much of Mexico by train.

I can count the days now until the trip. I keep socking away my money so I will have enough to cover me on the trip. It's only a few hundred dollars, but Chance assures me a hundred dollars in Mexico can buy what two thousand dollars buys in the States, and we will be fine. I hope he's right.

"Girl, I STILL wanna meet him"! Michael is jade green with envy about Chance. "He sounds too good to be true."

"Sorry, Michael, but he's kinda shy. He hasn't met my mother and I don't think he wants to meet my friends either."

"You're hiding him from me."

"Whatever, queen."

We're sipping cappuccini outside the Peet's coffee on the corner of Jackson and Fillmore, pretending to belong to the line of cashmere cardigans. When Conard House does its coffee walk, we march right past Peet's, past Sweet Inspirations, and into the Rolling Pin Donuts on California and Fillmore. It's a lowbrow establishment in a high-rent district, same as its counterpart on Castro Street. Today, I want to pretend I don't belong to coffee walk. Today I want to be part of the glamorous set haunting Jackson Street and Cow Hollow. I want to be rich. I want to be one of the city lights.

"When are you leaving again"? Michael asks.

"The 15th. We have tickets to Mexicali, and then we're catching a train."

"That sounds so fucking romantic."

"Yeah, well it's strictly platonic so far. Very romantic."

We sip from our cardboard cups and drain them of the last of their caffeinated grog. "Do you want me to bring you anything from Mexico"?

Michael pauses to think about this. "Yes, a Mule-tooth necklace, please."

"Done." I don't know where they sell them, but I know I can find them.

"Are you gonna see any ruins? Like those big Aztec ruins near Mexico City."

"We're playing it by ear, but we are definitely going to Chiapas to see Palenque."

"That's where the chariots of the gods thingy is, right"? of course Michael knows about ancient astronauts.

"The tomb of Pakal. He looks as if he's strapped into a spaceship. We studied it in my Archaeology class at Columbia."

"I am so jealous."

"Come with us. Mexico is cheap."

"Do you realize after rent and the PG&E bill I have 30 dollars to pay for my groceries for an entire month"?

"Can't you work under the table somewhere"?

"I wouldn't jeopardize my SSI for that. Sorry. Without it, I am nothing."

"I'll bring you a mule tooth necklace. Stay here and keep San Francisco from falling into the ocean."

"Fine, bitch, I will." We both cackle like old hens.

CHAPTER 19 - WHIZ BURGERS

The last person I will tell about this trip is my mother. I will telephone her from the Greyhound station in San Diego. Not a minute sooner. Given enough time, she would stomp all over everything. She would make the entire thing about her. She will destroy the plans, tell all the counselors, sue Conard House, whatever she can do to get extra attention and make me feel small and angry. So she doesn't get to know about it. Michael G. Page knows about it - he's a much better mother to me. He supports my trip, although he's still suspicious he hasn't met Chance yet. I will try to arrange a meeting when we come back from Mexico.

Today I ride the 22 Fillmore to the Mission to go to Whiz Burgers on 18th and South Van Ness. It's my favorite junk food restaurant. Whiz Burgers is an old drive-in hamburger stand where they still have girls on roller-skates to bring the food to your car door. I don't have a car, so I order a Whiz Burger special at the walk-up window. It's a cheeseburger, fries and a strawberry shake. Behind me in line is a tiny girl I remember meeting in the Haight. Her name is Munchkin.

Munchkin wants a Mango milkshake, but Whiz Burgers

doesn't carry mango. I have to admire her pluck. "If I go and buy a mango, would you put it in a vanilla milkshake"?

Robin, the bald man behind the counter shakes his head. She settles on a banana shake. "It's the next best thing to a mango shake. Hey Ethan, what's up"?

She remembers me. I tell her I am in a halfway house because I lost my mind.

She is at a hardcore detox called Walden House next to Buena Vista Park. "I hate it," she confesses, "I can't get away with anything. They call me on all my shit. I just want to get high."

A few months ago, getting high would sound pretty good to me, but I have Mexico now, and it dampens the pain and emptiness that dope could kill. I don't want to get high right now. I tell her about my upcoming trip and she is super jealous.

"I want to go! Can I just crawl into your suitcase and fall asleep by accident"? We laugh and enjoy our milkshakes. I wish I had chosen banana instead of strawberry. We exchange sips and we agree banana is far superior. "You can taste the chunks of banana in there, but not the strawberry; it's all chemicals. And there are no chunks of strawberry at all." She has excellent taste.

Tonight it's packed at Sweet Inspirations. There is some Kubrick film about Vietnam playing at the Clay, and everyone comes out needing sugar and coffee. That's what we're here for. After splitting the tips, there's twenty dollars just for me. Life is good. Twenty dollars will buy two nights at a motel in Palenque. I can't wait to go. Christmas came and went, and we are staring at 1988 like a tsunami about to wipe out 1987. Good riddance. What a fucking awful year! If I had it to do all over again, I would do ANYTHING to stay sane. I would sleep and ignore the earthquakes in my bed. I would find a better job than the fucking Stud. I would steer clear of AT&T and ITT Technical institute. I would NOT go to the Library and I would avoid the Mark Hopkins hotel. I would shun Dennis Peron's weed, and I would not stand in the wind and let random thoughts blow into my head. The whole mess could have been avoided.

Mexico is what matters now. 18 days and counting. Chance will be discharged this week. I'm the luckiest guy in Pacific Heights. And I have 1,000 times less money than any given neighbor. The letter of Paul to the Corinthians springs to mind. Though I speak with the tongues of men and of angels, but have not love, I have become sounding brass or a clanging cymbal. And though I have the gift of prophecy, and understand all mysteries and all knowledge, and though I have all faith, so that I could remove mountains, but have not love, I am nothing. And though I bestow all my goods to feed the poor, and though I give my body to be burned, but have not love, it profits me nothing. And though I drive a Mercedes Benz and have a million dollars in the bank, but have not love, I am nothing. What I have with Chance is the closest thing to love I have ever known. It might be love.

My meeting with Janis is at 10am, but when I get there, I see Chance talking with her, laughing. He puts his hand on her knee in a flirtatious gesture. I am jealous. His flirting just hits me in the heart in a weird place. He will be discharged soon, leaving me to fend for myself. I have Mah Jong and I have Kathleen, although she is a little dizzy. I'm jealous Chance is hogging my time with Janis, too. She's such a cool lady. After about 15 minutes, I stop standing in the doorway and find a place to sit where I can observe them together without appearing needy.

Chance finishes with Janis. He holds me in a big bear hug. I look at the parquet floors and try to make sense of the dozens of geometric patterns on the floor.

"Hey, little buddy, I put your money in your duffel bag - inside pocket."

Kathleen walks past and says, "Ta brae nacht na bricht." That's a greeting reserved for night time, but I don't bother correcting her. She leaves her Gaelic book out in the common room, where I can flip through and try to learn a language so close to my own, and yet so foreign. I will stick to Spanish and French, the two I learned in high school.

Janis is already seeing another client, so I figure I can skip it for today. Chance notices my faint tinge of jealousy. I ask him "What did you two talk about"?

"You," he answers. "It was all good. She doesn't know about Mexico. I was just talking about what a great kid you are."

"Thanks." The jealousy is replaced with embarrassment. I always blush when people say good things about me. Reminds me of my mother bragging about me in a narcissistic glow of triumph. She has nothing to brag about today. Her son is psychotic and spending time recovering from a stint in the mental hospital. She can't put any positive spin on that. That's why she's being such a dick to me. I'm making her look bad.

CHAPTER 20 - LOST CHANCE

Chance didn't say goodbye. He's gone now, and I am alone in the room. I expected some ceremonial farewell, a long embrace, even though we will be together on a train in Mexico in just a couple of weeks. He just vanished. He didn't have much stuff, because I can't even tell if anything is missing in the room. I never saw him get dressed or read or do anything suggesting he had possessions. It's like he was never here. I walk downstairs to play Mah Jong.

Nobody in the Mah Jong game knows about me and Chance, so Tony Ha doesn't ask me why I look so blue. Most of us look blue most of the time, so there's nothing special about it. I win a hand with all four winds and two birds - which brings great praise but leaves me empty. Mah Jong is too easy. I need to learn how to play Bridge or one of those other games that requires skill. Mah Jong is 90% luck and the other 10% is all that makes the difference between a champion and a loser.

Sweet Inspirations is crowded. I keep hoping Chance will show up and surprise me. I want to introduce him to Damon and the others. They've heard about him. No visitors. Just an endless line of upper middle class Pacific Heights residents ordering caffe latte, mocha and cappuccino. If it were not so busy, it would be hard to hide my sadness. Customers don't notice. I can spare them the loneliness of being away from Chance.

I channel my loneliness and isolation into making the perfect layered latte. I even try to pour the espresso into the glass mug without leaving a stain on top of the foam, but it is impossible. The Italians knew this to be so, or they would never have coined a name for the macchiato.

When things slow a bit, Damon chats with me. "Ethan, you live just up the street. Do you live with your parents?"

"No. It's a bunch of roommates."

I can't blame Damon for the puzzled look on his face.

"It's on Jackson?"

"Yeah." I would love to change the subject.

"Do any of your roommates stop by here?" God Damon is nosy.

And then, as if on cue, in walks Tony, Helen, Bernadette, Mei, Kathleen and a few other Conard House clients. Tony swaggers as he approaches the counter.

"So Ethan, we convince Janis we do coffee walk here today! You happy to see us!"

I was raised by wolves, but I went to a good finishing school. I know it is always the right choice to follow the path of truth and kindness. It is the gracious thing to do. At the tip of my tongue are a number of choice words. It is my job to put them all together in the right order, discarding the hurtful and shameful ones. I fail.

I turn to Damon and say, "I don't know who the fuck these people are." No sooner do the words leave my mouth then there's a great pain in my heart. Tony's face is crushed. Helen Ka looks away, blinking back tears. Mei loses all expression on her face.

Kathleen, oblivious, shakes Damon's hand and proclaims, "Ta brae nacht na bricht!"

Liz defuses the situation by addressing Tony with respect, "What can I get you, sir?"

Tony shakes his head and looks at his feet before shuffling out of the shop. As the leader of coffee walk, the entourage follows suit. I eat deep regret salad with shame dressing and cruelty croutons.

At the end of the shift, Damon hands me an envelope.

"What's this"?

"It's your last paycheck."

I'm not clear if he fired me for being mentally ill or for being a dick. I think about it while I walk to the house. Either way, I deserved it.

Inside, I hear the clatter of Mah Jong tiles in the living room. I can't go in there. How can I face my friends after being such a cunt?

"Ethan, 'that you?" I hear Tony calling.

With trepidation I answer, "No, it's some asshole who acted ashamed of his friends."

"Good. We have one spot at table for asshole. Come sit your asshole down."

This is the best reaction I could hope for. I may be a dick, but Tony Ha is not. He is forgiving.

While we shuffle, Tony explains. "Ethan, this your first time in mental health right"?

"Yes."

"This my five times. You not ashamed of friends. You ashamed of yourself."

We stack the walls in silence. "I'm so sorry I treated you like that."

"We know because we all do it before." He says a few words in Chinese. Helen and Annie nod.

Tony continues, "We maybe do because of family or church or work. Normal. You know what important?"

I shake my head.

"You came back to table and play. You good person in

bad place."

I found an old copy of The Bell Jar in the library basement and read it cover to cover in one sitting. I laughed out loud. I know it's supposed to be a sad story, but she must have meant for it to be funny. She couldn't have known while she wrote it. She couldn't have known she would die in a sealed kitchen with her head in the oven. She seemed so hopeful.

CHAPTER 21 - SIXTH STREET

Michael G. Page is visiting today at Conard House. Tony comes to the room and tells me I have a visitor. Downstairs, there's Michael. He looks like a rat in a snake cage.

"Girl, this place is freaking me out. Where can we go? I know they're going to figure me out, lock me up, and throw away my keys. He curls his lip and titters.

I'm saving my pennies for Mexico, so I decide we should go to the coffee walk Rolling Pin Donuts on California. Michael says he doesn't care where it is as long as it has coffee.

In Rolling Pin, he grills me about Chance. "How come I haven't met him? How can I give him the Michael G. Page seal of approval? Tell me more about him."

"He has olive skin and green eyes. He has a motorcycle, and he works at a Vespa repair shop on Van Ness near the Marina. He's built like a brick shithouse. And he's bisexual."

"Yeah, you told me a month ago. Is he dangerous? Does he own a gun? Where is he now? I forget what you said."

"He's staying at a GA hotel on Sixth Street."

"Let's go there and find him. I want to see this Chance

for myself. You know I'm your real mother, and you need my approval before you hop a train to Mexico with a bipolar bisexual."

"Yeah, I don't remember which hotel it is."

"Well then we'll just have to try them all."

Sixth Street is the filthiest, loudest, most vile street in the City. Crack whores and petty felons line the street, looking for an angle on every passerby.

"Late night, satellite" echoes along the corridor. Bike messengers come here to buy weed, speed, crack and whatever else their measly paycheck can purchase. They are lucky if their bikes aren't stolen while they are busy copping drugs. This was a bad idea.

A man with a burnt afro and red-rimmed eyes walks into our personal space. "Late night, satellite, nice bag of water"

"Back off"! Michael wields a canister of pepper spray. The man doesn't even notice, just keeps walking, looking for his next prey.

"Michael, I know Chance is here somewhere, but he would be in his room staying out of this mess."

"This is fun, Ethan"! Michael is a kid on an Easter Egg hunt. "Now, why is it you don't remember which hotel it is"?

"They all sound the same. " It's true - most of the Hotels on Sixth street sound like some place fancy - the Regal, the Royal, the The Windsor, The Pontiac, The Balmoral Arms, The Whitaker, The Haven …none of them bears any resemblance to the fancy name. We stand at the Royal on Minna. I press the buzzer. The unpleasant Sikh man behind the counter looks startled anyone has disturbed his newspaper time.

"Hi, we're looking for Chance. Is he staying here"? I ask.

"Chance Who"? Good question. I am surprised to realize I don't know his last name, despite having shared intimate quarters with him for the last two months.

Michael raises an eyebrow when I fail to provide a last name.

"Girl, what in God's name are you planning a trip to Mexico for if you don't even know his last name"?

"It's just a detail; it never came up. He doesn't know my last name either." We step outside the Royal and Michael shakes his head from side to side. "I swear, the sooner you can get off those meds the better you will be. Two months and he doesn't know his goddamn last name. He could be a Getty, or he could be a gypsy, and you wouldn't know."

"Lay off. He's perfect."

Michael frowns, "I think you might be dick-ma-tized."

I should be angry, but the word is so absurd I just burst out laughing instead.

We take refuge from the abhorrent face of humanity inside Tu-Lan, an ancient Vietnamese restaurant whose menu boasts an amateur sketch of Julia Child. Legend states she comes to Tu-Lan whenever she is in town, Sixth Street notwithstanding. We order Vietnamese iced coffees, which come in the form of a tall glass of ice with sweetened condensed milk at the bottom, topped by a metal drip device that delivers powerful coffee in tiny droplets into the glass below. The drip process takes ten minutes, then it is ready to stir.

Michael looks at me while he stirs and chats. "I think Chance is too good to be true. How is the sex"?

"Um."

"You haven't fucked? I keep forgetting you're a Pisces. See it's hard for us Scorpios to imagine a non-sexual love relationship. It gives me the creeps."

"We'll have time in Mexico." I wonder to myself whether this trip will be chaste torture or a fuck-fest. I bet on the former.

We sip in silence for several minutes, the loud crashes and bangs from the kitchen punctuating the otherwise peaceful retreat inside of Tu-Lan.

"Does he drink"? Michael is looking for the chink in the armor.

"Not a drop."

"How did he land in the happy house with you"?

"He tried to give a speech from the rotunda railing in City Hall."

"What was the speech about"?

"Gay marriage, among other things."

"Gay marriage? He sounds insane." Michael clucks his tongue. "That's all he did to get locked up"?

"Well, I'm not clear on all the details, but the cops thought he was trying to jump."

"Suicide? Bitch, you got yourself a drama queen. It's a good match for you. Just remember, I'm as batty as they come, and I never tried to kill myself."

"He's done with that."

"Yes, puss-puss, I wasn't saying he was still suicidal. It's just a darker form of mental torture, that's all. I can't talk to boys, and he wanted off the planet. It's a big difference."

"I see aliens. Where would that fall on the spectrum"?

"In between. Just be careful of his dark side, Ethan."

My iced coffee is just melted ice now, and I have to make a couple of embarrassing slurps to capture the last of the caffeine trapped at the bottom of the glass.

CHAPTER 22 - NO CHANCE

Today is the day I announce to Janis my plans to go AMA (Against Medical Advice) on a trip to Mexico with Chance. The meeting is set for 10am, like all my meetings with Janis. Tomorrow I meet with Chance and we will catch our bus to San Diego to start our trip. I have over eight hundred dollars saved up, which should be more than enough for a month in Mexico. The Peso is in crisis - it dropped again today, so the dollar is magic paper there. While I wait downstairs for my meeting, the pay phone rings. Tony answers it and says it's for me.

"Who is it"?

"Huh? I don't know."

"Is it Chance"?

"It's a lady." Shit. My mother.

I go to the phone and lift the receiver to my ear. My mother's voice is twisting my intestines from the inside.

"Ethan, we need to go see your Grandma tomorrow." Shit shit shit. How do I get out of this.

"I have to work tomorrow."

"Tell them you can't make it. I'm driving out to see Grandma Joe and I need you ready at 9 am outside Conard

House."

This call couldn't have come at a worse time. Whatever her agenda is, I can't use work as an excuse. Even though I lost my job, and she doesn't know, I'm furious at how she disregards my obligations. I swallow it.

"Mom, you know I love you and I love Grandma Joe, but work is important to me."

"Bullshit. What kind of crap are you trying to pull"? She puts a razor blade in the intestine. I'm out of options.

"Fuck off." I hang up the phone, which rings again moments later. I can see Janis' door is open now.

"Hey Ethan, do you answer the phone"? Tony is hovering. "I need to use it."

"Tell the lady I am in a meeting with my counselor, and then you can use the phone."

I run into Janis' office and close the door. She can see the look of distress on my face. Tony opens the door and leans in, "She really mean. She call me a name and tell me you have to talk to her."

I implore Janis with my eyes. She knows what's happening without any further words. In long strides, she crosses the entryway.

She talks into the pay phone. I can hear her using a calm, steady voice to talk to my mother. Her voice changes tone, and I can hear her say, "We don't allow that kind of language with our clients here." More silence, then, "He's in a meeting with me right now, so you can't talk to him." I can see the infuriated dragon-like expression on my mother's face when she hears those words. Janis leaves the pay phone receiver dangling and returns to the office, looking for a pen, paper and tape. She scrawls an "Out of Order" sign and tapes it to the phone, the receiver still dangling like a dead chicken head. From her office I can hear an angry squawking noise coming from the earpiece.

"Tony," she says, "use the payphone at the corner. This one is out of commission for a while." Tony trudges a resentful path to the front door and slams it shut behind him. Janis returns to her office and asks, "Now, where were we"?

This is the moment I have feared more than talking to my mother. Disappointing Janis is way worse, because I like her.

"Uh, Hi Janis."

"Hi Ethan. Your mother is being the usual nuisance."

"Yeah, she's kinda like that all the time."

"I'll bet it was pretty scary growing up with her."

"Well, I'm used to it now."

Janis pauses and gives me that 'therapy look' where she's waiting for me to say more. I don't take the bait this time.

"I have something different to discuss. Do you mind"?

"Sure, Ethan, this is your time."

"I am going on that trip I mentioned."

"Mexico"?

"Mexico."

"When?"

"Tomorrow."

"Ethan! Tomorrow? Leaving early is Against Medical Advice, as we discussed."

"Yeah. I know it's AMA. But it's sort of a once-in-a-lifetime opportunity."

"You should know you are giving up support from the Mental Health System. You won't be eligible for a Co-op apartment if you go."

"Yeah but I need this. I need to get away from the mental health system."

Janis leans in and whispers, "I agree 100%, Ethan, I just have to say all this crap to make it official AMA. Don't you dare repeat that!"

"I won't."

"It's a big trip to take by yourself. Will you be safe"?

"Yeah, well I'm going with Chance. Train trip." I wait for her to chastise me about relationships in the halfway house, but she doesn't.

“It’s a big risk. Still, you’re young; you have most of your marbles. You will be fine. But once again I am obliged to tell you your doctor won’t approve.”

“Pablo Morales can suck my dick.”

Janis grins and asks, “Will you bring your meds with you?”

“Maybe Cogentin or Ativan. Not Lithium. Fuck that shit.”

“I’m not a doctor and I can neither advise for or against your plan. Sorry, I have to say this stuff during these sorts of conversations. Go on.”

“Yeah, I get it, no problem.”

“You planned this trip all on your own. Are you sure you can handle Mexico on your own”?

“Well, it was Chance’s idea.”

“Who"?

“Chance. Anyway, we bought the tickets a couple of weeks ago.”

“Who’s Chance"?

“Chance, my roommate.”

“You mean Calvin"?

This is strange. “No, Chance, my other roommate, the one you discharged last week. You must remember him. I saw him in this very room flirting with you right before he was discharged.”

“Ethan, you live in a double room with Calvin. You were flirting with me a week or so ago, which was odd but amusing. You said you were bisexual.”

“No, that was—“ Reality smacks me so hard, I see stars. I grasp at them.

“Chance, He’s....not...”

I can’t see Janis now, because I am overflowing with tears. I panic. I grab at a box of Kleenex like it could hold back the misery and loneliness I just uncovered. I look outside the door, and there stands Chance, waiting in the wings. He isn't real and he isn't going with me to Mexico. He grows blurry then vanishes as my eyes pour forth an ocean of despair.

"Ethan, I can see you're in distress. Would it be okay if I give you a hug"?

I reach out like a mewling baby and bawl into Janis' sweater.

"He was so perfect! He was so perfect"!

"Who"?

"Nobody. Me. I made him up and believed my own lies"!

Janis would need to ask a dozen questions to understand my distress. Instead she just hugs me and lets me soak the shoulder of her sweater.

He must be real. He must. I can't stand feeling this alone for another second. I spend the rest of my half-hour crying and blowing my nose. Janis just lets me have my feelings.

I run upstairs to the room and look at my duffel. I got it at an army surplus store on Market Street. It is green canvas, with leather straps, and a dozen pockets inside and out. Piece by piece, I put my dirty clothes into the backpack. I take the blanket my Dad gave me and shove it into the backpack. I take my used booklet of 20-cent postcard stamps and shove them into my backpack. I take my bus tickets and shove them into the backpack. I take my whole crappy life possessions, of which there are precious few, and I shove them into the backpack. I open Grandma's tea leaves and pull out the wad of cash, and I shove it in there too. I glance at the dresser and see the Capodimonte statuette of Chance on his Vespa. I fling it across the room where it shatters into a hundred pieces.

I walk downstairs and out the front door, silent and unnoticed. I don't know where to go. Michael G Page would just gloat and tease me, and would have nowhere to put me. My mother would just send me back to Conard House. I have nowhere to go. I walk down Fillmore past the fancy shops with expensive furnishings I will never afford. I cross Geary and I'm in the bad neighborhood now. I don't care. Nobody approaches me. I must look dangerous.

I cross McAllister Street and head into the Lower Haight. Wanda lives here with Sue. They can help me. Wanda and Sue got a new place on Laussat Street. It's small, but maybe they have somewhere to stash me for a bit. I just need to be somewhere safe where I can cry and figure stuff out.

CHAPTER 23 - THE PINK SOFA

Wanda opens the door and sees me and pulls me to her bosom. "Ethie, what happened"?

"I…uh…broke up with my boyfriend and I need somewhere to cry."

"You can cry here all day if necessary. Here, come sit down." She escorts me to a gigantic pink womb of a sofa. "Do you need some privacy? I'll be in the kitchen doing a tarot reading with Sue."

"Hi Ethan"! Sue calls out from the kitchen. I try to answer back but sobs come instead.

"Ethan says Hi"! Wanda covers for me. "Now just lay your head down and let those tears out." She plants a stern blue clinical box of Kleenex on the coffee table. Somehow I expected the Kleenex to match the couch. I guess shopping choices are limited in the Lower Haight. The harsh blue snaps me out of my tears and now I'm angry. Angry at Chance, which I guess means angry at myself. He was just another Betsy. He made me believe I was loved and then he took it all away. I could never love myself the way Chance loved me.

I lie on the soft pink couch and stare at the glow-in-the-dark stars stuck to the ceiling. On the edge of my vision, I can see Betsy's wheelchair. I turn away and close my eyes. I don't need her bullshit right now.

"Hey Time Traveler."

"Go Away, Betsy."

"You can love yourself like Chance loved you, you know. You already did."

"It's not the same as having someone."

Wanda comes into the living room. "Did I hear you call, Ethan"?

"Sorry. I'm working through shit out loud."

"Don't be. You're safe here." Wanda returns to the tarot reading in the kitchen.

Betsy rolls backwards into the shadows and fades away. Good. I'm alone now, just me and my private thoughts. I am hollow, empty, as if I was still on Prolixin.

The couch continues to give way under my weight. The bearded clam pillows topple and cover me. In this moment, engulfed in pink comfort, nothing can harm me. Nobody can pierce the safety of this giant fluffy fortress. I drift into a dreamless oblivion of much-needed rest.

The safety and comfort are shattered by the telephone. I hear Wanda speaking to my mother.

"Yes, he's here. He's very upset, and he's napping on my couch."

The pause is filled with short gasps as Wanda faces the wrath of my mother.

"I didn't realize it was a prison. Aren't the inmates allowed to leave and visit friends"?

More invective from my mother comes spewing out of the receiver.

Wanda is firm. "He is napping now. If you want to pick him up, I will call you with the address at 7pm. He needs his rest. He's heartbroken." She slams down the receiver. It rings again once, but she turns off the ringer.

Wanda pokes her head in the living room to check on me, and I feign sleep. I can't deal with any of it right now. Sue wanders in and says, "He looks like an angel fast asleep."

Wanda affirms, "How he managed to survive his mother this far is a mystery to me. That woman would tear the wings off of angels and burn them with candle wax."

Sue says, "Let's cast a spell of protection for him."

"Great idea." They wander back to the kitchen and rummage around for ingredients. The adrenaline levels subside, replaced with a soft generalized dread, and before I know it, I'm asleep again.

After a few hours, Sue comes to my couch to comfort me. Why did I kiss her all those months ago? I don't understand my heart. It needs replacing. Sue is a lovely human being, adorned with red locks and wise glasses. But I prefer lads to lasses. Love is cruel and unforgiving. I know I have crushed Sue's heart just as as love crushed mine when Chance appeared and disappeared. I don't understand. I don't understand anything.

"Sue, I'm sorry I hurt you."

"I'm a fag hag, Ethan. Getting hurt is what we do," Sue reminds me.

"I prefer the term 'fruit fly.'"

"Oh,you do"? She reaches for my love handles and tickles me. I spazz and cry out for her to stop.

"But seriously, Sue. I spent the last two months in a relationship with someone who doesn't exist. What is wrong with me"?

"You know, he probably does exist on some other astral plane. Or right here," she points to my heart.

"I wanted you to meet him. His name was Chance. I thought you would like him."

"I'm sure I have met him, and I'm sure I did like him."

"He wore a black leather motorcycle jacket, and he had pale green eyes. When he held me, I felt safe. The kind of safe when you fall asleep in the back seat of your parent's car while they are driving. You know"?

"Yes. I do know. Although my father was bipolar and a really bad driver." She chuckles remembering. "I think I had a dream about Chance, and that's where I met him, Ethan. He's not on this plane, but he's with you."

"You believe that"?

"Don't you see visitors all the time? People who are with you but they aren't there?"

I remember Betsy. "Yes, I do."

"So do I. It's a side effect of being an empath."

"Chance was perfect."

"Listen to yourself. That name, Chance, it's so prophetic."

"I bought a ticket to Mexico. Well, to Calexico. What should I do"?

"In accounting class,we called your ticket 'sunk costs.' It's money you already spent and won't recover, so you shouldn't include it in any decisions going forwards. It is no longer relevant to decisions about the future."

"So what are you saying"?

"I'm saying, if you can afford to go to Mexico by yourself, and you want to go, you should just go. And if you can't afford it, or you don't know how to make it work by yourself, don't sweat the money you spent on any tickets, because it's already gone."

She has a good point. My bus leaves tomorrow morning. I could always go back to Conard House and return to my room and my same unbearable life. I could catch the bus to Mexico and spend my hard-earned Sweet Inspirations money on a trip of a lifetime. The fact I bought the tickets shouldn't matter. What matters is what I want. And I want to go to Mexico.

CHAPTER 24 - STRANDED

I clear out of Wanda's place before 7pm rolls around, so she could invite my mother to come over and look for me if it came to that. I think about the Greyhound station, which is a well-known entryway into the hell realm, and debate crashing on the floor there. They would kick me out for vagrancy and for not being a bum. But it's worth a try.

I head to the Greyhound station to see if my ticket will work on an overnight bus to San Diego. No dice. Gotta wait til morning. I rent a locker for a dollar and stash my duffel.

There is very little to do in this part of town that doesn't involve glass pipes, pickpockets, and eczema. I would go to Tu Lan for spring rolls, but they roll down the security shutters before the shadows grow long and darkness creeps in. This part of town is terrible during the day - at night, it is the 9th circle.

To amuse myself, I walk past the Fascination parlor to see what lost souls remain at this hour. It looks like a fluorescent-lit nursing home common room.

Then there is the Strand, an art house theater in both senses of the word. Most days, they play revivals, such as

"Alien" or "The Conformist." But Thursdays are gay porn night. And it's Thursday. I am trying to save my US dollars for pesos, so I don't run out of money, but the Strand is dirt cheap, and I can't resist putting on 3D glasses to watch Jack Wrangler in "Heavy Equipment." It's not for the porn, I tell myself, but for the once in a lifetime opportunity as an artist to see a 3D Gay porn film. This may never happen again. Admission is $2.50, and the double feature runs until 1am. The second feature is a 2D classic - Kansas City Trucking Company. I am 19 now, old enough to go in without being hassled. This could be a great escape from a broken heart.

Inside, things are not as artistic as I had imagined. I prefer the back row for a 3D movie so I can see the objects leaping out over the audience. But the back row at the Strand on gay porn night is reserved for a different purpose. There are dozens of men standing backs to the wall with their flies open, dozens more kneeling to face them on their cushioned seats, and many more shenanigans too dark to see in the flickering light of the 3D movie. This kind of sex terrifies me. I was raised on Byron, Shelley and Keats. I crave love, passion, art, romance. I don't want sex to be meaningless.

And where the fuck are the ushers? I have my answer when I see a man holding a flashlight on the receiving end of a blowjob. This is a crime, I am positive, but the perpetrators are all complicit and there are no victims. Except for the guys who get AIDS. Just thinking about that disease destroys any arousal I might have allowed myself. Instead, I am filled with an inexplicable mixture of anger, disgust, self-loathing, pity and fear.

I'm not letting the sex party on Row A ruin my 3D movie. I sit in Row E which is as far back as I can go without implying I want to be a part of the action. I'm hungry and I want popcorn. Kansas City Trucking is still on, so I won't miss the main feature. Again, every dollar spent this side of the border is a wasted motel in Mexico, so I choose the small, which only costs $1.75. I say 'only' because even though it is 3 or 4 cents worth of popcorn, it is still less expensive than the ridiculous popcorn at the Galaxy which costs $3.75 for a small!

The guy behind the counter is not cute, and he knows it. He has long stringy locks of greasy hair, Charles Nelson Reilly eyeglasses, and an ill-fitting three-piece suit. I'm judging the shit out of him. I don't say anything, because I feel as ugly as he looks and I might even be that ugly, so I just practice being polite. He doesn't cruise me. I hope he's straight. I'll bet he hates Thursday nights at the Strand. I could ask him, but a conversation with a creep is not part of my plans. Then he asks me a question.

"You don't look gay. Why are you here"?

"First of all, I am gay. I don't go near the back row because it disgusts me, but I am gay."

The popcorn vendor nods and waits for the rest.

"I'm here because how many times in your life will you have the chance to see a gay porn film that managed to raise enough capital to be produced in 3D? It's the sort of chance that only comes along once. Why are you here"?

"Well, I work here. And I'm not very gay."

That last bit is perplexing. What is 'very gay'? What is 'not very gay'? I don't want to be sucked into a conversation with this greaseball, but my verbal diarrhea erupts like a spastic colon of questions.

"How gay are you"?

"So, like, I'd do it with a pretty boy like you. I would. But not that guy." He nods in the direction of a 70's mustache clone, reaching into his 501's and adjusting his cock ring by the lobby mirror.

"You prefer women, right"?

"Nah. I like being alone. But you know, if you wanted to, maybe you and me could --"

"Let me stop you right there. I am flattered. I'm leaving

for Mexico in the morning. I'm here to waste some time until the bus leaves."

"A bus to Mexico? The Green Tortoise"?

"No, Greyhound."

"I got a place on 5th street if you want to crash there. No pressure, just you know, you can come over."

I notice a few worrisome details about the popcorn guy. First of all, he has a pentagram and a goat's head tattooed on the back of his hand. I don't know how I missed that. I also notice he wears a hunting knife in his belt. He could just be some wannabe survivalist Satanist. He could be a psychopath planning to bind, torture and kill me. Now I need to extricate myself from his hospitable tentacles before I find out how he uses the knife.

"Dude, where is the bathroom"?

He is dull-witted and doesn't even notice the deft change of subject.

The bathrooms are halfway up those stairs. There are no ladies here, so if you want privacy, you can use the ladies room.

I puzzle over his offer until I wander into the men's room, where every urinal is occupied. Hobos and businessmen stand side by side, stroking, looking, leering. I turn tail and head into the ladies room. After, I finish climbing the stairs, cross over to the left staircase, and tiptoe around the corner into the theater. Popcorn man doesn't see me.

Truth be told, "Heavy Equipment" is not a very well-constructed film. Jack Wrangler, the star, is very well put together, but the editing sucks. The thrilling 3D moments are pedestrian, like when he mops the floor and we see the mop from the point of view of the wringer. I had hoped he would let his humongous dick pop out from the waistband of his tightie whities, and it would graze the heads of the few audience members in front of me; this never happens. We never see any of the artistic sexual angles I had envisioned. We see a wrecking ball, the mop, a dump-truck dumping its load, but the sex is two-dimensional and humdrum.

The Strand will evict audience members at 1am, but I want to escape before I am forced to interact again with the quasi-serial killer popcorn vendor. At 12:15, Kansas City Trucking ends, and the final showing of "Heavy Equipment 3D" comes to life. I peek out in the lobby, and see Popcorn Killer selling stale Red Vines to a young Asian-looking man. There is a mutual attraction there. Hands touch, numbers are exchanged. I hightail it out of the Strand and onto Market Street. It's still early, so I head next door to the Starlight Lounge.

The Starlight Lounge is a pre-war bar. It is less gay than the popcorn guy. It's pretty much a 1 on the Kinsey scale. But it's so beautiful. The bar is horseshoe shaped, and the curving walls enclose it in a giant circle. The walls are decorated with hand-painted renderings of San Francisco in the 1930s. They are lit from below by colored lights. Neon green and gold lights curl across the ceiling.

The straight bartender demands my ID. I dig until I find the fake ID I bought in New York. It's a Massachusetts driver's license. Nobody ever knows what a Mass ID is supposed to look like, so it works. The ID is useless, I don't want to drink booze. I order a coffee.

"Irish Coffee"? The bartender doesn't meet many customers without a drinking problem.

"Plain Coffee, with cream, if you have it."

He grumbles and serves me the coffee.

"How much"?

He raises his hands, refusing payment. I whip a dollar out of my Velcro Madonna wallet and place it on the bar. He smiles at me. He wouldn't smile if he knew where I was ten minutes ago.

Nobody at the Starlight Lounge speaks to anyone else. It's not a pickup bar. It's a place where professional alcoholics go to hone their skills. It's a crack house for drinkers. I sit in silence, nursing my coffee. I am surprised with a generous free refill from the bartender; no tip accepted.

Last call comes sooner than I expect. I realize I have mistimed things and now risk running into the Satanic popcorn vendor if I am not careful. As the bedraggled unwashed alcoholics stream out of the bar, I join the stream, watchful for the oily-haired predator. He is nowhere to be seen. The Strand is locked tight. He lives on Fifth, and I'm going to the bus station on Seventh, so I am in the clear. I enter the station and breathe a sigh of relief.

Passengers are permitted to sleep upright on the benches. The long wooden benches are separated every 3 feet or so with a humped inlay of brass just sharp enough to make sleeping lengthwise impossible. I try putting my shoes over the brass hump, but it only compounds my discomfort. I have the thin blanket from my dad, but it's locked away for now. It would not be able to cushion the bump enough to allow for rest anyway. So I sleep upright, nodding off and waking when my neck softens to the point my head collapses forward onto my chest.

In desperation, I try to sleep in Child's pose. My knees are tucked under my chest, arms pointed behind me. I am a dung beetle. This works until the weight of my torso against my knees prevents my lungs from drawing enough air. I also realize I am presenting my rear end to every passerby. I need to adjust.

Sideways, I can't hold the pose, and my legs fall off of the bench.

I wake to find myself lying on the concrete staring into the face of a station agent. Hands planted on his hips, he wears a dehumanizing frown.

"This isn't a hotel."

"Yeah, I know, but I'm catching the early bus to San Diego and I don't have money for a motel."

The agent reaches to help me to my feet, and plants me on the uncomfortable bench.

"What time is your bus"?

I peer at my ticket to remember.

"7:35 AM"

"Well, you got just two more hours. Try to stay upright on your bench until then."

"Yes, sir." I smirk and he walks away, filing my face in his mind among the unwashed horde of ne'er-do-wells and bums. This stigma will never go away. I struggle to earn a few hundred dollars here and there, but I know I'm fooling myself if I think I can support myself. Look what happened in New York. Look what happened in the Tenderloin and the hospital. I can't figure it out.

I don't have to figure it out, because I awake from a light upright nap and see the clock reads 7:00 am. I check the chalkboards at the front of each stall to see where the San Diego bus is. I find it, but the door is closed and locked. The driver stands a few yards away, smoking a cigarette.

"We board at 7:20." and he blows a puff of smoke.

After retrieving my backpack from the locker, I head to the restroom to splash some water on my face. The sinks only provide cold water and the only soap is Boraxo. The mirror is made of once-shiny stainless steel, scarred by knife marks, but it still provides a cloudy distorted reflection. I massage the pebbly powder with some water until it forms a feeble imitation of lather. I rub the abrasive concoction on my face to remove the oily sheen from my face. I rinse, avoiding stray grains of this quasi-soap from getting into my eyes.

When I survey my work, I catch a terrifying glimpse in the mirror. It's Satanic Popcorn guy from the Strand pissing at the urinal. He hasn't seen me yet, I hope. The knife attached to his waist is bigger than I remember. This Greyhound bathroom is the precise place where murders happen.

I back away from the mirror towards the door, keeping my eye on the knife and its owner reflected in the scratchy metal mirror. He doesn't see me.

Just as I reach the door, he turns and looks straight at me. He hasn't bothered to put anything away or zip up.

"Where did you think you were going"? he asks. He's stroking himself one handed, the other hand on the hilt of the knife. "I have been watching you for hours. You are so pretty when you sleep."

Just then, a gargantuan man in a uniform whacks the door open. He sees the popcorn dude with his dick out and smells trouble.

To my relief, he flashes a badge and tells Popcorn guy to put it away. Then he looks at me.

"What were you two doing"?

My first instinct is to just duck under his arm and run for the bus. But I already know what happens when you try to run away from a cop. You're guilty until rendered innocent.

Popcorn guy is still fumbling with his zipper, so I concoct the story.

"He was asking me for directions to Union Square, and he must have forgotten to zip his pants."

The oversized cop narrows his eyes. I see my open window and talk my way out.

"My bus is leaving in a few minutes, and my parents are expecting me. I need to go to Aisle 7."

"Where are you going"?

"Mexico. I mean San Diego."

Damn. The cop is glaring at me.

"My family live in San Diego, but we're going on vacation to Ensenada."

The cop brightens up. "Ensenada - the jewel of the

Pacific. The fishing is excellent. You're in for a real treat."

"Yes, sir, I am."

"You sure this guy wasn't bothering you"? He indicates Popcorn with a jerk of his head.

I must answer the cop now, but for several nanoseconds I debate telling the truth. This guy is a wannabe serial killer and I was about to be his next victim. But I keep it simple.

"Not a bit, officer. It was just an honest mistake. I know I've done it before." I force a chuckle and smile. "Haven't you"?

The cop frowns, "No. I put things back in my pants where they belong. And I don't make a habit of talking to strangers in the bathroom. It's not normal."

I'm done protecting my would-be killer, so I beg off. "So may I go catch my bus now? My little sister would be heartbroken if I didn't see her before bedtime."

"Yeah, okay."

I don't look back, hightail it out of the restroom and head straight for Aisle 7, where the driver is just unlocking the door. A handful of passengers have formed a line, and I put myself in the back of it. Every second ticking by makes me think the cop will let Popcorn go and I'll be abducted. My rational brain tells me abducting someone in daylight in front of a dozen witnesses is not realistic. My limbic brain has other ideas. I'm in a spiral of fight or flight. I fumble in my backpack for Cogentin and swallow one dry.

Three people are behind me in line, and I'm only a few steps from the coach door. I'm safe. I look over my shoulder, and see Popcorn skulking away. He doesn't approach me; I am free.

CHAPTER 25 - THIS WAY TO MEXICO

As soon as I slump into my seat near the back of the bus, I curl in a fetal position with the window and aisle seats as my feather bed. Nobody sits this far back, so no one is there to complain. I learn why no one sits at the back of the bus. The restroom smells like an outhouse. On Maslow's hierarchy of needs, sleep trumps olfactory distress. The smell makes me nauseous, but I don't vomit, so sleeping in the stink zone is the better choice.

I don't know how many hours have elapsed, but the coach appears to be somewhere in the Central Valley. We drive past 100 miles of dormant fruit trees, vineyards, almond blossoms, and Cowschwitz aka Harris Ranch. The combined scent of megatons of manure and the well-used bus toilet bring me very close to the vomit zone, but I retch and retreat as the cows fade behind us in the distance. Once my stomach settles, it admonishes me it is empty. I realize there is no food aboard a bus, and I forgot to buy anything in The City before we left.

I find my way to the front of the bus. The driver points to the sign "No unnecessary conversation with the driver." I'm not sure how to gauge this on the necessity scale, but it would be at the base of Maslow's pyramid.

"Sir, I can see you are very busy so I'll be quick. Where do we stop next"?

"Bakersfield in two hours."

"Will there be time to disembark and buy some food"?

"No, there won't."

I thank him and head back towards my stinky seat when a wrinkled brown arm reaches out and grabs me. The arm is connected to an ancient Mexican woman in a colorful poncho who beams at me.

"Tienes hambre, mijo"?

"Si, mucho hambre." I'm very hungry.

She digs into her bag and produces a foil package for me.

"Es un burrito"? I ask.

"No, es tamal de pollo." It's a chicken tamale.

"Cuanto"? I reach for some bills in my pocket, but she puts her leathery brown hand on mine and shakes her head.

I fight back tears. This is the first kind gesture anyone has shown me since I left Wanda's house. "Grácias no seria suficiente para expresar mi gratitúd." I say, stringing my word beads with vocabulary gleaned from García Lorca. She is impressed I was able to put together such a complex sentence, and compliments me on my Spanish. I beam as I tell her I am going to Palenque and I will need to be even better in Spanish. At least I think that's what I am saying.

She motions me to lean in, then kisses me on the forehead and says, "Que Dios te bendiga y te proteja en tu viaje."

I return to my seat and peel back the layers of foil, paper, and corn leaves so I can devour the tamale. It's delicious. The chicken is just the right amount of spicy without burning my tongue, and the masa is oily and firm, with no lumps or dry spots in the middle. I can see the old lady looking back over her shoulder towards me. I raise the tamal in salute, and smile so wide, she can't miss it. She smiles back. Thank heaven for small mercies.

After the Grapevine and a winding pass through the Angeles National Forest, we descend into the chemical warfare pea soup smog belt of the San Fernando Valley. Visibility drops; eyes water. This is Los Angeles. It is huge. You could fit Manhattan into a single neighborhood of Los Angeles. In Frank Lloyd Wright's vision of Utopia, everyone has a house with land and a driveway. Los Angeles is the embodiment of Wright's ideal. Le Corbusier, a rival architect, pictured people living in close quarters, with layer upon layer of public transportation between buildings. He saw Hong Kong, Manhattan, San Francisco. In Los Angeles, tall apartment buildings are only found in a few places. Unlike home, there are only a few apartment buildings downtown taller than 12 stories. I remember reading somewhere there was a law stating buildings could not be higher than City Hall. When the ban was lifted, it was during the growth of big business. Skyscrapers are commercially zoned in Downtown Los Angeles. The biggest population lives on Skid Row in giant cardboard cities. Los Angeles abandoned its center and created a dozen smaller centers. And there is no subway, so every journey requires a car or a two-hour bus trip. Traffic crawls on the 5, and houses sprout in clusters of poison mushrooms. I have heard Los Angeles is beautiful, but from where we are parked on the Interstate, no proof can be seen. If I could see further than 100 feet, I might see something beautiful. I know there are mountains and tall buildings nearby, but they are lost in the dark brown mire.

I have to switch buses in downtown LA. If I thought the San Francisco depot was bad, it cannot hold a candle to the chaos, corruption, crack and crank cementing this place together.

The San Diego bound coach is already taking passengers; I can climb aboard to remove myself from the beggars, fallen women and thieves who call this station home.

We leave the smog behind us as we traverse Orange County. In San Clemente, we reach the ocean, where the beauty returns and intensifies. Despite nuclear power plants and military bases, the road to San Diego belies a beauty reminiscent of the descriptions the Padres made when they first built El Camino Real. As we enter the San Diego urban sprawl, there is none of the dire ugliness glimpsed in Los Angeles. It's more Disneyland than Detroit. The air is clear, buildings gleam, and every street has a Spanish name. I'm on a boat stuck in the Mexico section of "It's A Small World."

The Greyhound depot is the only ugly thing in San Diego. I can see why my friends who grew up here have such happy faces and sincere smiles. The shining golden streets are criss-crossed by silver trolley tracks. The sunset over Coronado inspires the same awe as the fall foliage in Vermont.

I make the connection to the bus to Calexico. In the old days, the buses used to cross over the border into Mexicali, but things are not so easy any more. After a winding trip astride the mesas, we pull into a squalid town lined with drought-tolerant cacti growing from salty grey sand. This is Calexico.

Heffernan, the street leading towards the border, is lined with money exchanges. My pack is heavy, but not too much to handle. The border is at least a half-mile from the bus depot. As I pass the various money exchanges, I notice the different ways they gouge their customers. Some make it look as if you get 3,600 pesos to the dollar, but there is a 7% commission on the back end, so it's really only 3,350. Another advertises 3,500 pesos to the dollar with a $17.00 service fee (in fine print). I settle on the house offering 3,600 pesos with a 2% commission and a $5.00 flat fee. I keep 100 US dollars in reserve, and exchange all the rest for pesos. I need a wheelbarrow to carry the money. It stresses the seams of my duffel. I spend 20 or 30 minutes rearranging my gear so the money is stashed in multiple places, all of them out of sight.

Out in front of a restaurant called Pollo Grande (Big Chicken) is a person dressed as a big chicken, spinning a sign reading "Full chicken dinner for four - $10.99" and "Mexico Car Insurance". The chicken approaches me.

"Do you need Insurance"?

"I'm not driving."

"We have traveler's insurance." The chicken is a skilled salesperson.

"What does it cover"?

"In the event you are killed while you are in Mexico, your family receives $50,000.00"

"Anything else? Like if someone robs me, can I get my money back"?

"No, nothing like that. Just death."

"Thanks, I'll take my chances."

"Are you hungry, my friend"?

I am. He escorts me into the fluorescent glare of the restaurant. The menu hangs from the wall, grubby and limited, I settle for the five dollar special, two pieces of chicken with French fries. When the food arrives, it surprises me in several ways. First, it is delicious. The skin is crispy without being dry. The fries are the thick kind you see at a fancy steakhouse like Cattleman's. Plus, without any warning, the meal includes Spanish rice, whole pinto beans, and a foil wrapped stack of corn tortillas. San Francisco makes you pay extra for this kind of stuff. Here in Calexico, it's all included.

I underestimated just how far I would need to walk. A young boy in a pedicab pulls beside me. "Going to the border, Mister?"

"Yes. Is it far?"

"Hop on."

"Dude, I am counting pennies. How much?"

The kid shrugs. "How about a buck?"

For a faggoty trip with a rickshaw boy, one dollar is a bargain. I climb aboard. "What's your name, kid"?

"Juan. But I go by John."

Juan careens through the dusty streets, until traffic forms a blockade his pedicab could never penetrate.

The border is within sight. I can see a large Mexican flag, and a series of tollbooths, topped by giant cement letters spelling out "Welcome to Mexico." I give Juan two bucks and he pedals away.

So this is it. Chance convinced me to make this journey with him, then became a figment. Now I stand here alone at the crossing. I have no idea what to expect. Do they search your bags? Do they insist on bribes? Each step forward brings me closer to finding out.

The gateway to Mexico is flanked by a chain link fence. From a distance, the fence has shrubs growing through the links, but as I near the border, the shrubs come into focus. They are the hands of a hundred children. Their little arms reach through the fence, grasping for anything they can take from America. A simple chain link barrier severs the first world from the third.

I come to a plaza marking the last remnants of the United States. I expect hundreds of people in line to enter Mexico; I am the only person in the plaza. No one wants to go to Mexicali at this hour.

There are bilingual pedestrian arrows pointing "This way to Mexico | a Mexico." There never was any doubt as to which way to go. It's obvious where to cross. There is no one waiting to frisk me or demand information here in the United States. I guess nobody has a problem with people leaving. I ascend a concrete set of steps. At the top of the steps is a brass plaque: "Boundary of the United States of America.

Just past the plaque is a one-way revolving metal gate. I become a piece of cheese in a grater as I press forward, through the gate, crossing the barrier between two worlds.

ABOUT THE AUTHOR

Duncan MacLeod is a native Californian who was transplanted to the East Coast for boarding school and a failed semester at a prestigious Ivy League school. He returned to California to finish his education at San Francisco State University, where he majored in Film and Italian. He directed a feature documentary about Mexican wrestling called "La Lucha/The Struggle," performed lead autoharp in the band "The Acres," and is author of the semi-autobiographical Psychotic Break Series, starting with 5150. Half is the second installment. Currently, he lives in greater Los Angeles with his partner Rafael and his dog Patsy. M3X1(0, the third book in the series., will be available in early 2018.

Made in the USA
San Bernardino, CA
04 March 2019